ROCK HARBOR
# SEARCH
## &RESCUE

# ROCK HARBOR
# *SEARCH*
# *&RESCUE*

## by Colleen Coble
### and Robin Caroll

THOMAS NELSON
*Since 1798*

NASHVILLE   DALLAS   MEXICO CITY   RIO DE JANEIRO

Published in Nashville, Tennessee, by Tommy Nelson. Tommy Nelson is a registered trademark of Thomas Nelson, Inc.

Thomas Nelson, Inc., titles may be purchased in bulk for educational, business, fund-raising, or sales promotional use. For information, please e-mail SpecialMarkets@ ThomasNelson.com.

Unless otherwise noted, scripture quotations are taken from the Holy Bible, New International Version®, NIV®. Copyright © 1973, 1978, 1984, 2011 by Biblica, Inc.™ Used by permission of Zondervan. All rights reserved. www.zondervan.com

**Library of Congress Cataloging-in-Publication Data**

Coble, Colleen.
    Rock Harbor search and rescue / by Colleen Coble and Robin Caroll.
        pages cm
        Summary: "When an expensive necklace is stolen from a renowned jewelry artist at Rock Harbor's fall festival and Emily is accused of the crime, it looks like she'll never get her puppy and be able to join the Rock Harbor Search and Rescue team. Emily sets out to find the real culprit"—Provided by publisher.
        ISBN 978-1-4003-2106-3 (pbk.)
        [1. Search dogs—Fiction. 2. Rescue dogs—Fiction. 3. Dogs—Fiction. 4. Mystery and detective stories. 5. Christian life—Fiction.] I. Caroll, Robin. II. Title.
PZ7.C6355Ro 2013
[Fic]—dc23                                    2012044586

*Printed in the United States of America*

13 14 15 16 17 RRD 6 5 4 3 2 1

To Remy and Bella . . . because your input ROCKED!

 **ONE**

"I don't think he's got a scent." Emily O'Reilly waved away the black flies that swarmed around her face. Their search dog, Charley, had paused and was nosing a patch of leaves. The trees blocked out the sun here and made her shiver.

Her stepmother, Naomi, paused to catch her breath. "It's going to be dark soon. Mrs. McKinley will be frantic if we don't find her dog."

Emily glanced around at the dark shadows. "I hate to think of little Chloe out here." She loved her neighbor's little poodle. She cupped her hands around her mouth. "Chloe!" Only the wind answered her. Tears pricked her eyes. They'd been searching for over two hours. What if an owl had carried off the puppy? Or, even worse, an eagle?

Naomi put her hand on Emily's shoulder. "Don't look like that, Emily. We'll find her."

If she were only five instead of nearly fourteen, Emily would have buried her face against Naomi and cried. "What about predators out here?" she whispered. She could hear rustling in the woods around her. She knew it was probably squirrels or birds getting out of the way of the search-and-rescue team, but it was easy to imagine a fox or a wolf instead that may want to have a poodle-sized snack. Or could it be the Windigo? The thought of the old Ojibwa legend made her throat tighten. She'd been lost out here once when she was a kid, and the noises she'd heard in the night still came back to haunt her.

Or maybe it was her imagination. She *knew* the Windigo was only a legend—the Ojibwa Native American tribe's version of a bogeyman—but it was still enough to give her goose bumps. Her babysitter had told her the old story enough times that Emily could never forget it. And even though she knew better . . . out here, in the dark, with the wind moving through the trees . . .

"She's probably just wandered off," Naomi assured. She called Charley to her and had him sniff the bag that held one of Chloe's stuffed animals. "Search, Charley!"

The dog whined, then put his nose in the air and leaped over a fallen log. He began to bark. His tail went up, and he disappeared into the shadows. "He's got a scent!" Naomi shouted. She took off after the dog.

Emily ran hard to keep up. *Please, God, let Chloe be okay.* Her heart raced, and she strained to catch a glimpse of the dog. There was a yip, then she heard two dogs barking. One was clearly a small dog from the frantic yapping. "Chloe!"

The leaves rustled, and Chloe burst into view. Emily fell to her knees, and the sweet little poodle ran straight to her arms. Her little pink tongue lapped at Emily's face. "You're all right!" She didn't care if she was crying. She hugged the dog and turned her wet face up to Naomi. "I thought an owl had gotten her." She swiped at her eyes with the back of her hand and then stood up with the dog in her arms.

Suddenly, Naomi's cell phone softly began playing the theme song from *The Princess Bride* inside her jacket, and she answered it. From this side of the conversation, Emily realized there was another problem. Her gut tightened when Naomi hung up and called Charley to her.

"A couple at a nearby camper reported their ten-year-old son hasn't come back from a short hike along a well-marked trail," Naomi said. "I'd rather not pull you into this, but we're closer than anyone else."

"I want to help!" The dog wiggled in Emily's arms. "What about Chloe?"

"The sheriff is heading this way with a scent article. We'll give Chloe to him."

"We just wait here?"

Naomi nodded. "Sheriff Kaleva is on a four-wheeler. He'll be here any minute."

Emily tipped her head at a distant noise. "I think I hear him now."

Darkness was falling quickly, and moments later headlamps pierced the dimness of the forest. A burly form dismounted from the machine and came their way with a paper bag in his hand.

The sheriff held out the bag. "The little boy's sweater is in here. His name is Xander."

"How long has he been gone?" Emily asked.

"A couple of hours. The parents looked for him first before they called me."

Naomi took the bag. "We'll start right away."

Emily handed Chloe over to the sheriff. "She's tired and hungry, I think."

The sheriff tucked the small dog under one arm and turned back toward the four-wheeler. "I'll have Mrs. McKinley meet me at the campground."

When the roar of the engine faded, Naomi knelt beside Charley and opened the paper bag so her dog could sniff it. Charley thrust his nose into the bag, then ran around the clearing with his nose in the air. The search dogs were all air scenters. They followed as he ran off into the woods.

Darkness had completely enveloped the deep woods. Emily got a flashlight out of her ready-pack. While she had paused to grab it, the beam from Naomi's light had vanished. "Naomi, where are you?"

When silence answered her, Emily's gut tightened. She hadn't counted on being alone in the dark. Not after remembering the Windigo legends. When something rustled off to her left, she broke into a panicked run. Her breath tore in and out of her throat, and her lungs burned. She had to get out of here!

She stumbled over something and sprawled into a mat of leaves and spruce needles. The sharp scent of pine cleared her head. She sat up and felt around for her flashlight. Her hand touched on the metal, and she flicked it on. No reassuring light beamed out. She shook the casing and tried again. Nothing. She was out here in the dark by herself. With the Windigo.

Something howled in the distance. She hoped it was Charley, but what if it wasn't? What if the Windigo was coming for her? She scrambled to her feet and shrieked Naomi's name. The fear in her voice ratcheted up the panic in her chest.

"God's here with me," she whispered. "Nothing can hurt me."

She'd always been told not to move around if she got lost, but everything in her wanted to rush away from the night sounds echoing around her. She backed up until her rump was against a tree. A little boy was lost out there. She needed to be strong and let Naomi find the kid. Then Charley would come for her.

It seemed forever that Emily stood there trying to identify every sound in the dark. The strength in her knees gave out, and she sank to the ground. She'd never been so terrified. How long had it been? Half an hour? Two hours? She had no way of knowing.

Something rustled in the bushes again, and she lifted her head. A cold nose touched her hand.

*Charley!*

She threw her arms around his neck as Naomi stepped into view.

"Emily, why didn't you follow me?" Naomi asked.

"I stopped to get my flashlight, then couldn't find you."

*Sheesh*, Emily thought. *I sound like a baby instead of thirteen.*

"I mean, I knew you'd come back for me. Did you find Xander?" Emily struggled to her feet.

"I did," said Naomi. "I texted the coordinates to the sheriff, and he picked him up. He's probably back with his parents by now. I told Charley to find you, and he led me straight back here."

Emily didn't want to admit she'd been terrified, so she brushed the leaves from her jeans. "I was pretty lame, wasn't I?"

Naomi smiled. "You did exactly what I've always told you to do—stay put. You've got a knack for search and rescue, Emily. I think it's about time we thought about getting you your own search dog."

"Really? My birthday is in a few weeks," Emily said hopefully.

Naomi's blue eyes were warm. "Your dad and I think you should earn half the money to buy it. Bree has some puppies she'll be selling soon."

Emily gasped. "One of *Samson's* puppies?" Samson was one of the best search dogs in the country. She hadn't dreamed she could own one of his pups. "It would take me years to earn enough."

"I've already talked to her, and she's saving one for you at a very discounted price."

Bree and Samson were one of the most famous canine search-and-rescue teams in the world. Search and rescue was just about the coolest job Emily could think of.

Emily flung her arms around Naomi. "Thank you, thank you! You're the best! How much will the dog cost?"

"Three hundred."

Emily's elation faded. How could she earn a hundred and fifty dollars? Babysitting didn't pay that well.

*My necklaces.* Good thing the Rock Harbor Annual Fall Festival was coming up. Emily had a booth reserved to sell some of the jewelry she'd made. If she sold enough pieces, she could totally earn that hundred and fifty dollars. She vowed right then to make as many pieces as possible before the festival.

People from the surrounding counties and states crowded the downtown streets for the annual Fall Festival in Rock Harbor. The town had been settled by Finns back in the copper mining days, and it still held the flavor of its residents. This September morning, the booths and tables lining the sidewalks and streets held many Finnish wares. Rugs, pottery, furniture, thimbleberry jam, and copper items decorated both sides of Houghton Street. The aroma of beef pasties and Finnish rye bread filled the air, making Emily's stomach growl.

Bree Matthews walked toward her, and Emily's gaze immediately went to the puppy in her arms. She could hardly breathe when Bree stopped and smiled. "Like him?"

"He's *sooo cute*! Is this one going to be mine?" Emily held the puppy up to her face, and the tan fur ball nipped at her chin. "You won't sell him to anyone else, right?" She put every bit of appeal she could muster into her expression as she looked at Bree.

Bree nodded her head. "I'm holding him for you. I brought him to the festival so he wouldn't be lonely. His siblings are for sale at my booth. All but one has already sold."

"I love you, Bree," Emily said fervently.

Bree's green eyes twinkled. "I hope you loved me before I saved you a puppy."

"Always!"

"I need to get back to my booth," Bree said. "Kade will be wondering what's keeping me."

Emily sighed, pressed a kiss on the top of the puppy's head, and then handed him back to her. Bree walked away with the dog peeking over her shoulder. It was all Emily could do not to chase after her. She turned away and glanced around the downtown area.

People dressed in Finnish clothing milled around as they prepared for the parade. Emily was really impressed with the outfit Olivia Webster, her best friend, wore. An orange wool vest covered Olivia's blouse with its full sleeves. The orange-and-black skirt had a herringbone pattern, and her headband matched the skirt. The color looked good against Olivia's pale skin and brown hair. Olivia had made it herself, spending as much time on it as

Emily did on her jewelry making. She admired Olivia's talent. When Emily tried to sew, the results were a mess.

"I bet your parents are sorry they didn't get to see you wear your costume," Emily said.

"Mom was really disappointed. But they made the plans for the cruise before the town changed the date of the festival. And besides, I get to stay with you." Olivia slumped beside Emily as they sat behind the jewelry booth. "What are you going to name your puppy?"

"I haven't decided yet. I'll need to find the perfect name for him." She nudged her friend. "Did you see Mary Dancer's jewelry? I think I did pretty well copying her Sapphire Beauty necklace, the one to ward off the Windigo." Saying the word made Emily shiver and glance around.

Olivia picked up the fused glass necklace from the table next to Emily's booth and examined it. "I think you did too. It's a little smaller than hers, but the color is similar." She set it back on the velvet display. "I don't know why you like her stuff so much. It's a little plain. I like more sparkle." She batted her eyes at Emily, and the two girls burst into giggles.

Mary Dancer approached Emily from the other end of her booth. She was way old, at least fifty. She wore a long red skirt, a leather vest, and several of her own necklaces.

"Hi, Mrs. Dancer," Emily said. "You've had a lot of customers."

"It's been a good morning." She pressed her hand to her stomach. "I-I'm not feeling very well. Would you girls look after my booth until I get back?"

The woman did look a little green. "We'd be glad to." Emily crossed the grass between the two displays. "We'll try to snag you some more customers too!"

8

Mrs. Dancer's smile was more of a grimace. "I'll be right back." She darted across the street toward the bathrooms.

Emily wandered along the display. "I love her stuff." If only she could make jewelry as good as Mrs. Dancer's. She'd have the money to buy her puppy sooner rather than later.

"We know how you love it. Trust me, we *all* know," Olivia said.

A few customers stopped by both booths, and Emily sold a red hawk necklace and a pair of earrings from Mrs. Dancer's stock. She carefully tucked the money into the metal box, then moved to her table to sell a black onyx necklace.

A tall young woman approached, several people following her. Emily gasped as she recognized her. "That's Malia Spencer," she whispered to Olivia.

"Wow, I heard she was coming for the big surfing championship in a few weekends." Olivia squinted toward the group of people passing. "I thought all surfers were younger."

"Well, she won the women's world championship this year. It probably takes time to get that good."

The famous surfer stopped to talk to three boys who were in the surfing club. Emily was so busy watching them that she didn't notice two customers at Mrs. Dancer's table until the man cleared his throat. She hurried to assist them and sold them a necklace. By the time she had completed the sale and stored the money, Malia had moved on.

She stared after the surfer. "I wonder if Josh knows she's here." Though she'd watched for him, she hadn't seen Josh yet. Surely he would be here if the women's world champion was making an appearance.

"Emily has a *cruuu-ush*," Olivia said in a singsong voice. "You might at least talk to him sometime."

Emily flopped onto a folding chair, her cheeks burning, and sighed. "What's the use? Dad won't let me even look at a boy until I'm sixteen. That's two years away. He'd lock me in my room if he thought I liked a boy." But Josh Thorensen was way cute.

"Two years and a month," Olivia corrected.

"But my puppy will be mine in a month." Emily sat up and grabbed her bag. She checked her money. "I've made almost one hundred and twenty-five dollars so far."

"How much do you have to make?"

"Dad and Naomi are paying half of the cost for my birthday. So I need to earn a hundred and fifty." She was a little annoyed that her dad thought she needed to prove she was responsible enough to own a pet. As if she hadn't proven it over and over already. Her little brother, Timmy, had diabetes, and when their mother left them when Emily was only eight, she had managed to take care of him and the house, hadn't she?

That was before Dad married Naomi. Three years ago they'd had Emily's second little brother, Matthew. Didn't she help with babysitting him? How much more responsible did she need to be?

"The festival is going on all weekend. I bet you'll make all the money you need." Olivia smiled and nodded to her left. "Look who's here."

Emily's chest tightened at the sight of a familiar shock of blond hair. Josh even *looked* like a surfer with his thick hair, blue eyes, and lean build. But her stomach plunged when she saw who stood beside him.

Rachel Zinn.

Though she and Rachel were both in the eighth grade, Rachel was the kind of girl who was born knowing how to talk to boys.

She had the classic look: straight and silky blond hair, big blue eyes, and a short and petite build. School had just started, and already she was the head cheerleader of the junior varsity team and the president of the eighth-grade class. Not to mention her incredibly wealthy father sat on the city council and owned the fishing resort. Emily always felt invisible when Rachel was around.

They used to be friends, and Emily still wasn't sure what had happened.

For the millionth time, Emily wished her hair wasn't so curly and that she didn't stand so tall. She seemed to tower over all the other girls in her grade. But even more, she especially wished the curves she'd already gotten weren't so obvious. It was embarrassing.

She shrank behind her table and let Olivia talk to them as they looked at the pieces of Mrs. Dancer's jewelry. But Rachel didn't miss Emily. She smiled, put her arm through Josh's, and hollered out, "Oh, hi, Emily." Her smile did nothing to hide her smugness.

Josh barely glanced in her direction.

Heat burned through Emily as she looked their way. She gave a little wave, then ducked under the tablecloth and pulled out the small plastic bins with the leather cords she used for the necklaces. Maybe Rachel and Josh would leave if she kept busy.

Rachel laughed at something Josh said, then tugged him toward the enticing beef pasties booth.

Emily could finally breathe when they walked on down the sidewalk.

"You could have at least talked to them," Olivia said.

"I was busy."

"Yeah, right." Olivia nodded across the way. "Here comes Mrs. Dancer. She'll be excited to know how much we sold for her."

The woman's color was better as she came toward the table. "Thanks for taking care of things for me. Looks like you sold a few things." Her smile faded when she looked down at the display. "Did you sell my Sapphire Beauty?"

"No, it's right here." Emily knew the piece well. It was the one she'd copied. But when she picked up what she thought was the expensive necklace, she knew it wasn't right. It was too light. And small.

It was also *her* copy.

The valuable piece of Mrs. Dancer's jewelry was gone.

The Saturday morning went from bad to worse really quickly.

Emily sat behind her own booth, Mrs. Dancer pacing behind hers. Dad and Naomi stood on Houghton Street's curb, whispering as they waited for Sheriff Mason Kaleva to return. Mrs. Dancer kept staring at Emily with every pass, and she didn't smile.

Surely Mrs. Dancer knew Emily had no idea what had happened to the prized Windigo necklace. She had to know.

Olivia fidgeted in the chair beside her. Olivia didn't have a clue either.

Sheriff Kaleva returned, stepping behind the tables and motioning for Dad and Naomi to do the same. "Mary, let's start with your statement."

Mrs. Dancer's hand rested against her stomach. "I haven't been feeling well this morning but have had a steady flow of customers. When I needed to use the facilities, I asked Emily to watch my booth. She agreed. I was gone maybe fifteen . . . twenty minutes,

and when I returned, my necklace was gone, and this imitation"—
she held up the necklace Emily had made—"was in its place."

The Kitchigami County sheriff turned to Emily.

Before he could say a word or ask a question, she jumped to
her feet. "I have no idea what happened to her Sapphire Beauty."

"Calm down. Let's take this one step at a time. Did you see anyone near that particular necklace while Mrs. Dancer was away?"

Not really. Well . . . Josh and Rachel *had* been standing in that
area. Emily turned to Olivia. "What was Rachel looking at when
she and Josh were here?"

Olivia stood and shrugged. "She was more interested in making sure you noticed she was with Josh than looking at anything
on the table."

Emily's face burned, and she avoided looking at her father. If
he thought she was interested in a boy, when he'd gone on and on
about her being too young to notice boys . . .

"Rachel who?" asked Sheriff Kaleva.

"Zinn." Emily crossed her arms over her chest.

"Jacob Zinn's daughter?" Dad asked.

Emily nodded, still not looking at him.

"Anyone else stop at the table?" Sheriff Kaleva continued.

"A lady bought a necklace and earrings of Mrs. Dancer's. I put
the money in the metal box." Emily pressed her lips together and
tried to remember.

"Oh, and that couple," Olivia said.

The sheriff shifted to face her. "What couple?"

"When Malia Spencer came by, we were watching her, and we
didn't notice a man and woman at Mrs. Dancer's table until the
man cleared his throat."

Emily picked up where Olivia left off. "I rushed over to help them. They were looking at several necklaces, and I finally sold one of the red ones."

"Were they looking at my Sapphire Beauty?" Mrs. Dancer asked.

"I don't know. They were there, and the special display is right in the center, so I guess they saw it." She shouldn't have let herself be distracted by Malia Spencer. It wasn't as if she cared about surfing herself. She was terrified of going in Lake Superior—she would never put so much as a toe in there. Josh was the one really interested in surfing.

Maybe Dad was right and she *was* too young to notice boys.

Sheriff Kaleva turned to Mrs. Dancer. "Mary, when was the last time you know you saw your necklace?"

"Half an hour, maybe forty-five minutes before I let Emily watch my booth. I showed it to Lucy Cooper."

Emily twirled her hair around a finger. Mrs. Cooper's husband was in jail, and the family had moved away. The fact that they were back in town was big news to Emily.

"And that was the last time you saw it?" asked Sheriff Kaleva.

Mrs. Dancer nodded. "When I came back from the restrooms, this imitation of Emily's was in its place in the display."

The sheriff moved around to the front of the tables as people continued to mill about. Most had cleared for a spell before the noontime parade began.

"Emily, where was your copy of the necklace when you last saw it?"

She pointed to the center area of her table. "There. Between those bracelets."

He glanced at Emily's table, then Mrs. Dancer's. "Did any of you notice someone stopping at both tables?"

They all shook their heads.

The sheriff closed the little notebook he'd been writing in and slapped it against his palm. "We'll do our best to find the necklace, Mary, but at this point, there's not much we can do."

"That was my most expensive piece, Sheriff. It's worth at least a thousand dollars." Mrs. Dancer glared at Emily. "Why don't you check her boxes?"

Emily's heart skipped a beat. "Wh-what? You think I took your necklace?"

"You were supposed to be watching my booth."

She wanted to cry and throw up all at the same time. "I didn't take it, Mrs. Dancer. I would never—"

The woman's eyes went even darker with accusation. "You made a copy of it. Why? Maybe you made it to switch them so you could steal my Sapphire Beauty."

"That's just crazy!"

"Now, Mary, we don't know what happened to your necklace." The sheriff stared at Emily. "Yet."

Now she really wanted to cry.

"We'll work the case and see what we can find." Sheriff Kaleva nodded at Emily's dad and Naomi, who stopped by the curb and spoke in hushed tones.

"I'm packing up and going home. The festival is ruined for me." Mrs. Dancer pulled her jewelry from the table and slipped everything in her cases. "I had that necklace blessed by the medicine man. The Windigo will strike while the protection is gone. Mark my words, Sheriff."

"I didn't take the necklace," Emily whispered.

Olivia put her arm around Emily's shoulders. "We know you didn't. Mrs. Dancer does too. She's just upset right now."

The sheriff left, and Dad came behind the table. He looked stern. "How much money have you made today?"

Emily handed him her bag of money as Naomi joined them. "Almost one hundred and twenty-five dollars."

Dad took the money and handed the bills to Emily. "I think you should give this to Mrs. Dancer."

"For what?" Surely this was some test of Dad's.

"That was an expensive necklace, Emily."

Her hands shook. "I didn't take the necklace, Dad."

"But you were watching her booth. You were responsible for it."

Her eyes burned. "Dad, for all I know, that necklace had been switched before I ever watched the booth for her."

"Emily, this isn't up for discussion."

She marched over to Mrs. Dancer and handed her the bills without a word. Tears burned her eyes as she returned to her booth. What about her puppy?

"Get your things. It's time to go home. Go get Matthew and Charley from Bree's booth. We'll meet you at the truck."

Emily blinked away the tears as she threw her jewelry into the bins.

"It's going to be okay," Olivia whispered under her breath.

No. It wasn't going to be okay. Emily wasn't going to have the money to pay Bree for the puppy. Even worse, everyone, even her own dad, thought she'd taken the necklace.

She wasn't a thief.

She wasn't.

# TWO

"Olivia, will you please excuse us?" Emily's dad's voice was stern, and he didn't smile.

Emily looked at her hands. Wasn't giving all her money to Mrs. Dancer enough punishment?

"Yes, sir." Olivia shot a sympathetic look to Emily, then headed down the hall to Emily's room. Charley skidded down the hall behind Timmy, Emily's younger brother, and Naomi, who carried a sleepy Matthew.

Emily crossed her arms over her chest and shifted her weight from one leg to the other, then back again. She couldn't explain the feeling inside, only that she felt sicker than ever.

"Sit down," Dad ordered as he sat in his recliner.

She plopped down onto the overstuffed couch, grabbed the old throw pillow, pulled it into her lap, and pressed it against her stomach.

"Mrs. Dancer is really upset, and rightfully so. That was a very expensive necklace that's gone missing." Dad used that voice of his that made her feel like she was five years old again.

"I'm upset too. I didn't take the necklace, but you're acting like I did."

Naomi returned to the living room before Dad could say anything else. "Matthew was ready for his nap. He's already asleep, and Timmy's playing his new video game in his room." She moved one of the many books she had scattered around the house and sat on the other end of the couch, smiling at Emily. "Honey, no one is accusing you of taking the necklace."

"Then why is everyone treating me like I did?"

"The sheriff had to ask all those questions. He didn't say he thought you took it."

"Dad thinks I did. Otherwise he wouldn't have made me give Mrs. Dancer all my money." The tears burned her eyes again. She blinked them away, refusing to cry. "I almost had enough to buy my puppy."

Dad shook his head. "I didn't say I thought you took her necklace, Emily. What I said was that you were responsible for it. She asked you to watch her merchandise, you said you would, and it went missing while you were in charge of her booth. If you accept responsibility for something, you have to be held accountable for it." He inhaled and frowned. "So I'm going to have to let Bree know we aren't buying the puppy."

Emily jumped to her feet, her whole body shaking. "Dad, you can't do that! It wasn't my fault. You promised!"

"Oh, Donovan," Naomi said. "Isn't that a little harsh?"

Dad shook his head. "Emily needs to learn about responsibility."

"Please, Dad," Emily begged. "Maybe the necklace will turn up. Don't let Bree sell my puppy to someone else."

Naomi looked at Dad. He sighed. "The puppy won't be ready

to be adopted for another month. I'll let it ride a while. Maybe the necklace will turn up. I hope so."

A month. She latched onto the sliver of hope. "It wasn't my fault, Dad. You'll see. I'm not a criminal." When his expression didn't change, her stomach tightened. "Oh, wait. My mom's in prison, so naturally I must be a criminal too. That's it, isn't it?" She wasn't going to be able to stop the tears.

She rushed down the hall.

"Emily—" Dad started, but Naomi interrupted. "Let her go. Give her some time to calm down."

Emily didn't hear the rest of Naomi's advice to her dad. She slammed her bedroom door behind her and fell face-first across her bed. She buried her face in her pillow as the tears escaped.

"I'm sorry," Olivia whispered.

Emily sat up and wiped her face. She hated to cry, but Olivia would never tell. "They think I took that necklace. I can tell. And even worse, Dad will tell Bree to sell the puppy to someone else if the necklace doesn't turn up."

"But you didn't take it!"

"Well, you and I seem to be the only two people who know that."

Olivia chewed her bottom lip. "What are you going to do?"

"I have to do something. The sheriff thinks I took it, so he's not going to be looking for who really stole it." Emily pulled her legs up and sat cross-legged on her bed across from Olivia. "I'm going to have to find the real thief."

"I'll help you." Olivia held her gaze, her face full of determination. "How are we going to do that?"

Emily thought about it for just a moment, then grabbed a spiral notebook and pencil from her desk. She hopped back onto the bed. "We need to make a list of everyone we saw by both booths. Remember, whoever took Mrs. Dancer's necklace had to take mine first to put in its place."

"Good idea." Olivia sat cross-legged across from her on the bed.

"Okay. First is Mary Dancer." Emily wrote the name at the top of the page.

"Why would she take her own necklace?"

"Don't you think it odd that she noticed it was supposedly missing *as soon* as she got back from the bathroom? She didn't even check the money first, just asked about the necklace. How'd she know it was swapped out so quickly?" Emily chewed the pencil's worn eraser. "My copy wasn't perfect, but it wasn't so far off that she'd take one glance at it and know it wasn't her necklace."

"True. But, again, why would she take it?"

Emily shrugged. "Maybe she took out a loan from someone she shouldn't have, and they're threatening to break her legs if she doesn't pay them back."

Olivia laughed. "You watch too much television, Em."

Emily grinned. "According to Dad I do." She slumped back against the headboard. "I don't know why she would take it."

Charley whined outside Emily's bedroom.

Emily threw a stuffed teddy bear at the door. "Shh, Charley. Go play with Timmy."

"Hey, is her necklace insured?" Olivia's mother worked as an insurance adjuster. "If it was insured, then she'd get the money if it was lost or stolen."

Emily gasped. "That could be it! So she might have a financial reason to take her own necklace. We know she had the chance to not only take her own necklace, but also to take mine to put in its place."

Olivia nodded. "And what was that she said about the Windigo striking?"

"She said her Sapphire Beauty would protect against the Windigo, so it probably has something to do with the legend." Emily shivered. "That old legend is scary. They're like vampires or zombies. What if Windigoes are where those legends come from? Maybe there's some truth to all of it." The wind howled around her window the way it usually did, but tonight she could imagine the Windigo howling for her blood.

"Who else?"

"Rachel Zinn." Emily wrote her name under Mrs. Dancer's.

"I don't know for sure she was looking at that particular necklace."

"She could have been."

"Why would she take Mrs. Dancer's necklace? According to her own words, Rachel doesn't wear *homemade* jewelry."

True. When she'd found out Emily made the trendy jewelry, Rachel made a point to tell everyone who would listen that *she* would never wear such *cheap-looking, homemade* jewelry.

Charley whined again. What was wrong with that dog? Had Timmy gone outside to play and left Charley behind?

"If she doesn't like it, why would she take it?" Olivia asked.

"To get me in trouble. It's no secret she doesn't like me. She could've taken my necklace and replaced Mrs. Dancer's with mine just to get me in trouble." She and Rachel had gone to school together since kindergarten, but ever since they started middle school Rachel had been nothing but mean to Emily.

"True."

"I don't know what she was looking at on either table or for how long because . . ." Heat flooded Emily's face again. She could only imagine how red it looked.

"Because you were watching Josh. I don't really know either . . . because I was watching you watch Josh."

"Okay, so that's Mrs. Dancer and Rachel. Who else?" Emily chewed the eraser.

"Em, if you list Rachel, you have to list Josh too."

Emily didn't even want to think about it. "Good grief, what would a boy want with a necklace?"

Olivia shrugged. "It's worth a lot of money. He's been talking about the Gitchee Gumee Surfers needing new equipment."

She had a point, but that didn't mean Emily had to like it. Nor could she ignore he'd been there. She scrawled his name under Rachel's and moved on. "Who else?"

"That couple you helped. The man looked annoyed that you weren't paying attention. We were watching Malia Spencer."

"But they bought something."

"So? That could've been to make them less of a suspect."

"Right. I don't know who they are. Do you?"

Olivia scrunched her nose. "The woman looked a little familiar, but I can't think of from where. Maybe it'll come to me later."

The dog pawed at Emily's bedroom door. "Did you know a Samoyed husky named Laika was the first animal in space?"

Olivia rolled her eyes. "Stop spouting off history facts and focus on the case!"

"Sorry, I've just been studying so much for History Smackdown that I've got a million facts swirling around in my head." Emily wrote down *The Couple*. "Go find Timmy, Charley." She chewed on the end of her pencil. "Oh, and Mrs. Cooper."

"I hadn't heard she and Pansy were back in town." Olivia

shook her head. "It had to be really hard on them to leave the only home they knew."

"Yeah, but I can understand why they left. People can be pretty mean." Emily couldn't believe Mrs. Cooper had come back to Rock Harbor after everything. She had to be either brave or desperate.

"I know. I feel sorry for Pansy. It's not her fault her dad stole the money from the town."

Yeah, and it wasn't Emily's fault her mother was in jail either, but it didn't stop people from whispering behind her back. "I feel sorry for them too. I know what it's like."

Mr. Cooper worked in the tax office, and he'd stolen tax money. When he was caught a year ago, he'd been sent to jail. Emily was a little vague on the details, but everyone in town had been talking about it.

"I overheard Mom and Dad talking right before they left on the cruise that Mrs. Cooper had just come back to Rock Harbor. Seems that she's having some serious money problems."

Emily grinned at her best friend. "You overheard? You mean, you were eavesdropping?"

Now it was Olivia's turn to blush and drop her gaze to the pretty pink comforter Naomi had bought especially for Emily's birthday last year. "I can't help it if their voices carry when they're talking so loud."

"What else did you overhear?"

"Just that she had enrolled Pansy in school and was looking for a job. So far, no one would hire her."

"I wonder if Bree knows." Bree was the sweetest woman ever, and if she knew no one would hire Mrs. Cooper, she would definitely try to help.

Olivia nodded at the list. "That's not many people."

"I know, but it's a start. It'll be more than what the sheriff is looking for."

"Do you really believe Sheriff Kaleva thinks you took the necklace, Emily?"

"He sure acted like it. And you saw the way he looked at me." She shivered. "Like he was ready to arrest me right there." For a minute, she imagined herself thrown into jail—in her mother's cell. The thought made her want to throw up, and she hugged the pillow. "I can't think about it."

Olivia nodded. "I'm sorry. We'll find out who really took the necklace. Then Sheriff Kaleva will have to apologize for even thinking you had anything to do with it."

Timmy spilled out of the closet. "Can me and Dave help?"

Emily jumped off her bed in shock. "Timmy! You aren't supposed to be in my room." At least that explained why Charley was acting so crazy. She'd busted her little pest of a brother time and again for being in her room without her permission. Dad promised to ground him the next time he did it. She started toward the door. "I'm going to tell Dad."

Timmy looked alarmed and jumped in front of her. "Wait. Let me help. I don't think you took the stupid necklace either."

Emily stopped. "You don't?" It was great that someone believed her, but she was pretty sure he was only supporting her because he wanted something. "Why not?"

"Because you wouldn't do anything to stop Dad and Naomi from letting you have that puppy, that's why."

True. She cocked her head to the side. "But why do you want to help me?"

He shrugged. "Because you're my sister."

"What else?"

"Okay, okay." He held up his hands. "Me and Dave are bored. His mom and Naomi are busy with the Kitchigami Search-and-Rescue Training Center and Matthew and the twins. And Dad's busy with the hardware store. Nobody ever lets us do anything. We're tired of being treated like babies."

Emily opened her mouth to tell him no and to order him to leave her room, then snapped it closed. So many times Dad hadn't let her go somewhere or do something she really wanted to do because he thought she was too young. She hated when that happened. It didn't seem fair to do the same to Timmy. She turned to Olivia.

Olivia shrugged. "Why not? We should take all the help we can get."

Timmy jumped up and down. "C'mon, Em. I promise we won't be any trouble. We'll do whatever you say. Please?"

That alone was worth letting them help. She grinned. "Okay. But you have to promise to only do what I tell you, all right?"

He nodded, nearly bouncing up and down. "Can I call Dave and tell him?"

"Yeah, but tell him not to say anything to his mom." Bree was one of the coolest adults Emily knew, but who knew how she'd feel about her son helping in the investigation?

Timmy nodded again, then ran from the room.

Olivia giggled and lay back on the pillows. "You sure made his day."

"I hope I didn't make a mistake." What if Dad overheard Timmy talking to Dave? What if Dave told his mom? Bree and Naomi were best friends, just like Emily and Olivia.

"I don't think you did. Who knows? Maybe they'll actually be helpful. I hope so, because I don't have a clue where to start."

"Me either." Emily plopped back down on the bed and lifted the notebook. Olivia was right—they didn't have many suspects and not much to go on with the ones they did have.

Olivia sat upright on the bed. "Hey, maybe Dave could get Samson out in the area where the booth was and do some sniffing around."

Well . . . that was something. "What would he look for? The necklace? Too many of Mrs. Dancer's items were there, and I'm sure they'd all smell the same."

Olivia's face scrunched. "I guess so."

"Hey, it was a good thought." She flopped onto the bed on her stomach. "We've got to find a clue somehow."

She didn't want everyone to think she was a thief. She wasn't. Emily just had to prove it.

"Mason. Come in." Dad opened the front door and led the sheriff inside. "Please, have a seat."

Emily froze at the kitchen sink, her hand tightening around the glass of water she'd ventured out of her room for. She tilted her head, listening down the hall. The water in the bathroom was still running—Olivia took the longest showers ever. She moved around the kitchen island for a better visual on Dad and Sheriff Kaleva. Her heart thumped against her ribs. Maybe they'd found the necklace, and this nightmare would be over.

"Where's Naomi?" the sheriff asked as he followed Dad into the living room. He sat on the couch, keeping his back straight.

"Reading to Timmy. He's been having a tough time getting to sleep some nights." Dad sat in his big, comfy recliner, opposite the couch.

"I'm sorry to hear that."

Dad shifted in his seat. "This late, I'm pretty sure this isn't a social visit."

The sheriff glanced over his shoulder toward the hallway leading to the bedrooms. "Is Emily around? I've interviewed various people regarding Mary's missing necklace, and I'd like to discuss some of their statements with Emily. And you, of course."

"Sure." Dad stood.

Emily set down the glass and stepped into the living room. "I'm right here."

Dad frowned. "Were you eavesdropping?"

"No, sir." Heat burned her face. "Well, I didn't mean to. Olivia's taking her shower, and I was thirsty, so I came to the kitchen to get a drink of wa—"

"Never mind. Come sit down." Dad's expression didn't change. Emily was sure he'd *discuss* eavesdropping with her again after the sheriff left.

"Yes, sir." She moved to sit in the other recliner beside Dad's. She wiped her slick palms on her jeans.

"Emily." Sheriff Kaleva gave her a look that made her want to fidget in her seat. "I've interviewed several people who stopped by Mrs. Dancer's booth today."

She nodded, even though her pulse was pounding so loudly in her ears that she couldn't concentrate.

"One of the girls you mentioned, Rachel Zinn, remembered something she heard you say."

Sheriff Kaleva's face was somber, and she clutched her hands together. "What?"

The sheriff leaned a little bit toward the edge of his seat. "She said she overheard you telling someone you'd copied that necklace specifically so you could swap it and make a lot of money."

Gasping, Emily leaped to her feet and stared at the sheriff. "That's a lie! I never said that."

Dad's frown deepened into the lines of his face—never a good sign. "Emily, why would she lie?"

She bit her lip and struggled not to cry. He couldn't actually *believe* Rachel, could he? "Because she hates me. I don't know why, she just does. Dad, you've got to believe me!"

"Emily, sit down." Dad looked tired, and he rubbed his head.

She slumped back into the chair, even though it felt like every nerve in her body sat outside her skin. "Dad, I didn't take the necklace."

Dad's eyes narrowed until they were little slits. "You expect us to believe Rachel told a flat-out lie to the sheriff?"

"But she *is* lying. I never said that, Dad. You have to believe me." She looked back at Sheriff Kaleva. "It's her word against mine. I'm telling the truth."

Dad looked at the sheriff.

The sheriff gave a slight shake of his head. "Emily, it's not just Rachel who told me. Another girl, Gretchen Siller, was with Rachel and said basically the same thing."

*What? No way.* Gretchen didn't have anything against her. Emily's throat was so tight she thought she'd choke. "They're both wrong. I didn't say that." A thought occurred to her. "Who did they say I said that to?"

Sheriff Kaleva met her stare head-on. "Olivia."

She straightened in her chair. "Oh good, Olivia will tell you the truth when she gets out of the shower. She knows that I never said that."

The sheriff glanced at Dad, then back to her. "While that may be true, I'm uncomfortable questioning a minor without one of her parents present."

"She won't care. She'll tell you Rachel's lying."

Dad shook his head. "Emily, Sheriff Kaleva is right. I wouldn't want you questioned without me."

"So you're just going to take Rachel and Gretchen's word over mine without even asking Olivia?" *Don't cry, don't cry.* "How about if she just tells you that I didn't say that? It wouldn't be you questioning her, just her telling you the truth."

Sheriff Kaleva shook his head as he stood. "That's the same thing, Emily."

He motioned to the door as Dad stood as well. Together, they reached the foyer. The sheriff's voice was lowered, but Emily could still make out what he said. "We'll keep investigating, of course, but I'm going to be honest with you, Donovan. All the evidence is pointing to Emily."

Her body began to shake a bit uncontrollably. Why was this happening to her? She hadn't stolen the necklace, and she certainly had never said she was going to do that. Why did Rachel hate her so much that she'd lie? And what about Gretchen? Why would she lie about Emily? They'd been friends since kindergarten. Well, then again, so had Emily and Rachel.

"Emily." Dad had shut the door behind the sheriff and stood facing her. "I want to talk to you, but I need to talk with Naomi first. Go ahead and wait in your room until we call you."

Tears burned her eyes. "Dad, I promise you, I never said anything about stealing a necklace. I didn't take it. I promise."

"Just go to your room, Em. We'll discuss this later."

She ran to her room and threw herself across the bed, just

as Olivia opened the bathroom door. A cloud of steam wafted behind her. "What's the matter?"

Emily rolled onto her back. She told her what the sheriff had said and how her dad had reacted. "He really believes I took the necklace. On purpose. And that I'm lying. Why won't he believe me?"

"I'll tell him and Sheriff Kaleva that you didn't say that to me." Olivia sat on the ottoman at the foot of Emily's bed. "I can't believe Gretchen said that too."

"Me either. I thought Gretchen liked me." She'd never even had so much as an argument with Gretchen, so why would she back up Rachel's story? Wait a minute . . . "I bet Rachel made her lie so the sheriff would believe her story."

"How could Rachel *make* her lie?"

"I don't know, but Rachel can be pretty mean."

A knock sounded on the bedroom door, then it creaked open and Naomi stuck her head inside. She wasn't smiling. "Emily, your dad and I would like to speak to you for a moment."

"Yes, ma'am."

Olivia reached out and grabbed Naomi's hand. "Mrs. O'Reilly, I don't know why Rachel and Gretchen are lying, but Emily never said she was making the copy of Mrs. Dancer's Sapphire Beauty to steal it. She didn't tell me she planned to take the necklace."

Naomi smiled softly. "Thank you, Olivia. You're a good friend." The smile fell off her face as her stare lit on Emily. "Come on."

Emily followed Naomi into the living room. Dad stood, not a good sign. He pointed at the couch. "Sit down."

She sat and looked down at her hands. *Please, God, let him listen to me.* Maybe he'd give her the benefit of the doubt. She *was* telling the truth, after all.

"Are you sure there isn't anything you'd like to tell us?"

His stern voice brought tears to her eyes. If her own dad didn't believe her, who would? He really thought she'd plotted and planned to steal the necklace and then had done it.

She lifted her chin and looked at him, willing him to see the truth in her face. "I didn't take the necklace, Dad." She let her focus shift to Naomi. "I give you my word. I'm not lying."

Naomi's expression softened. "You have to realize how this looks, Emily. If it was just one person's word against yours . . . but it's two."

"And Olivia told you I never said I planned to steal the necklace, so it isn't just my word against Rachel's and Gretchen's."

"There's no logical reason for them to lie, Emily." Dad's tone was harsher than she'd heard in a long, long time.

A lump the size of Lake Superior almost choked her. "I don't know why they're lying, Daddy, just that I'm telling the truth. That's all I can say. God knows I'm not lying. And if you believe them, then you're also calling Olivia a liar. There's no logical reason for me to lie either, you know. What would I do with Mrs. Dancer's necklace? I couldn't wear it or sell it with everyone knowing it was stolen. And why would I ruin my chances to get my puppy? You know how badly I want him."

No one said anything. It was like they all held their breath. The old grandfather clock in the dining room ticked, the sound bouncing into the living room as loud as a drum.

Dad sighed. "For the next two weeks, I want you home by five every afternoon. You are to help Naomi with dinner and with Matthew and Timmy. Even with Olivia here."

"Yes, sir."

"And unless we hear something different from Sheriff Kaleva, there will be no puppy."

Her heart broke. It didn't matter what she said. He didn't believe her.

And that hurt worse than not getting her puppy.

# THREE

The September sun beat down on the city as its residents spilled out of the Rock Harbor Community Church. People visited as they walked slowly to their cars. Emily and Olivia walked away from Dad and Naomi, who were chatting with the pastor just outside the church's doors. Dave and Timmy hovered behind the girls.

"What are you doing?" Emily asked her brother.

"We're waiting on you to tell us what you want us to do and how we can help."

As if she had any idea. Suddenly, it hit her. "Pansy."

"Huh?" Both boys wore confused expressions.

"Pansy Cooper is back in school. The elementary school. You two see what you can find out from her. Her mom saw the necklace before Mrs. Dancer asked us to watch the booth." They hadn't been in church, but Emily wouldn't want to go and have everyone stare at her either.

"Like what?" Dave asked.

She shrugged. What could they find out?

"See if you hear anything about their mom having money

problems or if they recently had some money come in." Olivia looked at Emily. "If she stole the necklace, she'd have sold it quickly to get the money she needed."

"Good idea." Emily turned to the boys. "Just make friends with Pansy and see what you can find out."

"Davy!" Bree, with one of his two-year-old siblings on each hip, called across the lot. "Come on. We're going to your grammy's for lunch."

Dave nodded. "We'll see what we can find out tomorrow." He sprinted toward his family.

Emily, Olivia, and Timmy headed toward Dad and Naomi, who were making their way to the parking lot.

"You know, one thing's bothering me," Olivia whispered.

"What?" Emily stopped and grabbed Olivia's arm to stop her, but waved her brother on.

"You copied her necklace, right?"

"Yeah. I thought it was pretty, and she'd shown it in commercials for the festival. I thought maybe I could sell mine cheaper and make some money." *That* didn't quite work out the way she'd planned. "Why?"

"I know hers was bigger and heavier, but you both used fused glass and similar beads, didn't you? I mean, she didn't have any real gems or anything, right?"

"Right. Mine was smaller and lighter, but we used the same stuff. And I hoped my lower price for the same look would help it sell quickly." Now she'd not only lost all the money she'd made from her jewelry, but she also lost the chance to sell her biggest piece since Sheriff Kaleva had taken her knockoff as evidence.

"What was the price of yours?"

"Fifty dollars."

"Mrs. Dancer told the sheriff that hers was over a thousand dollars." Olivia rubbed the end of her nose. "I'm just wondering why hers is so much more, if you both used basically the same materials."

"Because she's Mary Dancer, I guess." But now that she thought about it, Emily didn't think Mrs. Dancer's necklace was worth *that* much more than hers. "And maybe because people believe it will ward off the Windigo. You heard what she said to the police about the Windigo striking while the protection was gone. Everyone knows that Mrs. Dancer made the necklace to ward off the Windigo. She said she had the medicine man bless it."

"Mom said it was silly to believe in that stuff. You don't believe in the Windigo, do you?"

Emily glanced over to the car. Dad and Naomi were still chatting with some of their neighbors. "Of course not." But when she was alone in the dark and heard something outside in the woods, the thought of the Windigo sometimes scared her. "At least, not now. But some of the old Ojibwa members here in the Kitchigami area *do* believe in the Windigo. They make charms and stuff like that to keep it away."

"Mrs. Dancer claimed her Sapphire Beauty could do that?"

Emily nodded. "Naomi showed me the picture of the necklace, so I read the article in the *Kitchigami Journal.*"

"You know," Olivia began, "if Mrs. Dancer's necklace was featured in the paper, maybe someone planned to steal it all along."

"You're right. I didn't even think about that. I can't remember everything the article said. I was mostly interested in looking at the necklace."

"We need to get a copy of that paper."

"Right. It was about three weeks ago."

"Emily! Olivia!" Naomi called. "Let's go."

As they climbed into the third-row seat of the Honda SUV, Emily's heart held on to the hope her best friend had given her. She could almost taste the apology everyone would have to give her when she proved she had nothing to do with the missing necklace. And Rachel Zinn would have to give a special apology for lying about her.

And maybe Mrs. Dancer would give Emily back her money. That puppy would be licking her chin very soon.

Sunday dinner was always loud at the O'Reilly house. From the time they got home from church, Naomi needed Emily's help in the kitchen making pasties, which were little beef semicircle pies that people had been eating since the Cornish miners brought them to the U.P. Olivia talked to her parents on the phone. Matthew took forever to go down for his nap, and Timmy broke two plates setting the table because he kept playing with Charley. Naomi had finally put the dog outside.

Adding to the craziness, Grandma Heinonen and her best friend, Mrs. McDonald, joined them. Grandma wasn't their *real* grandma since she was Naomi's mother, but Emily loved her just like she was. Most times, when Grandma and her best friend came over for meals, Emily didn't care one way or the other, but today . . . today she sat right beside Mrs. McDonald.

Mrs. McDonald was the town's biggest gossip. As she waved a plump hand in the air, Emily noticed her fingers held so many rings it was a wonder she could move her hand. "Hello, Emily, dear. How is school starting for you this year? Aren't you a freshman? High school is such great fun."

"No, ma'am. I start high school next year." Emily wished she could look forward to it, but her stomach clenched every time she thought about moving to the other side of the school.

"Oh, you'll love it. Such a wonderful time." Mrs. McDonald turned and spoke to Grandma on her other side about her rosebushes.

Emily waited until Dad had finished praying over the meal, then handed Mrs. McDonald the basket of rolls. "Mrs. McDonald, did you know that Mrs. Cooper and Pansy are back in Rock Harbor?"

"Emily!" Naomi frowned.

"Sorry." Emily widened her eyes on purpose. "I didn't know it was a secret."

"Shh, dear. It's not a secret." Mrs. McDonald looked at Naomi. "She's been back in town for two weeks, the poor thing. Trying to rebuild a life for her and poor Pansy." She tsked as she spooned green dill tomatoes onto her plate. "I can't believe she came back here, of all places. Like the citizens of Rock Harbor would just welcome her back into our fold after what Pete did."

"Why did she come back?" Emily asked, ignoring Dad's frown.

"Why, dear, she had no other place to go. At least their house here is paid for. She's been renting it out all this time, but the last boarder moved on a few weeks back. She and Pansy can have a roof over their heads here, at least."

"Where is she working?"

"Emily! This isn't your business," Naomi said.

Mrs. McDonald shook her head. "The child's merely curious, Naomi. There's nothing wrong with curiosity. I, myself, have always been a curious person." She smiled at Emily. "Lucy hasn't found a job yet, my dear. She's looking for just about anything, from what I'm told. I imagine she's getting quite desperate by this time."

"That's enough." Dad glared at Emily before forcing a smile at Mrs. McDonald and lifting his tone of voice. "We shouldn't discuss someone else's private business."

Emily dropped her gaze to the pasties Naomi had made for lunch. She cut off a piece and dipped it in ketchup before taking a bite. The mix of hamburger meat, potatoes, and carrots with just the right amount of onions tasted so good. Emily wondered as she chewed. *So Mrs. Cooper is getting desperate, is she?*

*Desperate enough to steal a necklace to feed her kid?*

Although excitement raced through Emily at the possibility of proving her innocence, her stomach knotted at the thought of Pansy needing food. Or clothes. She remembered what it felt like to be different from everybody at school after her own mother was sent to prison. She wouldn't wish those times on anyone. Not even Rachel Zinn. It certainly wasn't fair for Pansy to have to go through that.

Her appetite momentarily lost, Emily made eye contact with Olivia across the table. They needed to do something to help Pansy. Maybe she could have Timmy stick up for her if anyone tried to pick on Pansy. He'd said he would do whatever she told him to, right? She'd have a talk with him tonight.

Mrs. McDonald stared straight at Dad. "Perhaps not. Maybe we should go straight to the source for such information." She nudged Emily. "So, tell me about this stolen necklace of Mary Dancer's."

Emily forced herself to swallow the bite. It went down dry, scraping her throat. She coughed and reached for her glass of milk. She took a long gulp.

"I didn't mean to choke you up, dear. I'm merely asking what happened." But Mrs. McDonald's expression clearly showed her interest. Whatever she found out would be repeated. Probably several times over too.

As simply as she could, Emily explained what had happened. "And no matter what anyone says, I don't know what happened to the necklace."

"Of course you don't. I'm sure no one thinks you do, dear," Mrs. McDonald said.

Emily glanced at Dad, who still frowned. He seemed to believe Rachel Zinn's lies over his own daughter's word. "Emily . . ." There was no mistaking the warning tone of his voice.

"I know, I know. But I'm responsible for it going missing because I was watching Mrs. Dancer's booth." She looked back to Mrs. McDonald. "But she was gone for only fifteen or twenty minutes. Thirty, tops. No one can be positive the necklace went missing while Mrs. Dancer was in the bathroom."

"My goodness." Mrs. McDonald looked at Naomi. "What does Sheriff Kaleva say about this? I understand he took everyone's statement."

Naomi shrugged. "He's looking into it, but didn't give much hope in solving the mystery or recovering the necklace. It was her prized necklace, the piece she'd gotten a lot of publicity over. She's so upset."

And if they believed Rachel's lies . . .

"I imagine Mary's more than upset. I bet she's beside herself," Grandma said. "She wouldn't even let me exhibit her Sapphire Beauty at the bed-and-breakfast at first. Then I assured her I carried more than adequate insurance on all items I have for sale." She owned the Blue Bonnet Bed and Breakfast on Houghton Street. It kept busy year-round.

"You sell jewelry?" Emily had never thought about asking Grandma to show her stuff.

"I do, but I only sell items created by local artists. I've exhibited several of Mary's pieces, sold quite a few as well, and never has she been so particular about a single piece as she was over her Sapphire Beauty."

"Why?" Emily blurted out, despite Dad's frown returning. Didn't he understand how she needed to solve the mystery? Didn't he care how important this was to her?

"I don't know. Maybe because it's currently her most valuable piece?"

"Emily, go ahead and start on the dishes," Dad said, clearly ending the discussion.

Emily couldn't help but wonder what it was about the Windigo necklace that made Mrs. Dancer so protective of it.

And who would risk stealing it.

# FOUR

"Who can relate to the heroine of the story?" Mrs. Lempinen, the English teacher, asked.

Emily barely paid attention as most of her classmates raised their hands. The historical story wasn't very interesting, and she *loved* history. A young woman, once a street kid, had stolen to survive before she became respectable and helped out other street kids. Emily would have been much more interested in the girl if she'd found a way to do the right thing without stealing.

But it was more than the boring story that was making Emily's mind wander. All day, people had stared at her funny and then whispered as she walked by. She didn't bother asking them what they were talking about, but she already knew.

The missing necklace.

The *Kitchigami Journal* had done a whole article about it. She'd seen the paper that morning before she'd left for school. The necklace's disappearance took up half of the paper's front page. There were quotes from Mary Dancer and Sheriff Kaleva, and while neither named her, they stated that "a replica of the

41

Windigo necklace, made by the young lady whose booth was right beside Mary's, was left in place of the valuable Sapphire Beauty." Everyone knew they meant Emily.

"Who here thinks the young heroine's thieving ways were justified?"

Rachel Zinn waved her arm.

Emily caught Olivia's stare and rolled her eyes. Rachel was such a teacher's pet. Emily couldn't wait to catch Rachel outside of class and confront her about the lie she'd told the sheriff.

"Rachel," Mrs. Lempinen called on her.

Slowly, Rachel stood. "While stealing is wrong, the heroine of the story stole food." She turned away from the teacher and faced the class. "She stole food to eat so she wouldn't die of starvation. She only stole to survive, not for profit." Rachel's stare landed on Emily. "Unlike *some* people."

*Of all the nerve . . .* Emily balled her hands into fists under her desk.

Rachel turned back to Mrs. Lempinen and smiled that fake, sweet smile of hers. "I think her actions were justified."

"Thank you, Rachel." Mrs. Lempinen waited for Rachel to take her seat. "Does anyone else have any thoughts they'd like to share?"

The bell sounded before anyone could raise a hand.

"Remember to study tonight for the literature test tomorrow." Mrs. Lempinen dismissed the class with a wave of her hand.

Emily snatched her notebooks from her desk and pushed against her classmates to the door. "Hey." She followed Rachel into the hall. *Stay calm.* She couldn't go one second more without knowing why Rachel had told the sheriff such a crazy story.

Rachel kept walking, her blond hair swaying as she moved.

"Hey, Rachel." Emily raised her voice and grabbed Rachel's shoulder. "I want to talk to you."

Spinning, Rachel jerked free of Emily's hand. "Don't touch me."

Emily put her free hand on her hip. "I want to know why you're spreading lies about me."

Rachel raised one eyebrow. "I'm not."

"Yes, you are. You told Sheriff Kaleva that you heard me say I planned to steal Mrs. Dancer's necklace, and that's an out-and-out lie. You know it is."

People stopped moving in the hall. They hung together in groups, watching. Staring. Good. Maybe they'd all find out the truth.

Rachel shrugged. "I heard you tell Olivia you were making a copy of Mrs. Dancer's necklace so you could take hers and make a lot of money."

Emily shook her head. "I never said that. Why are you lying?"

Rachel's face reddened. "I'm not making it up. You told Olivia that in the girls' bathroom several weeks ago. I heard you. So did Gretchen." Rachel crossed her arms over her chest.

"I never said I planned to steal the necklace." Emily gripped her notebook tighter against her chest with her left hand and balled her right into a fist at her side. "I said—"

"You're just like the woman we read about. But worse. You didn't steal for a good reason. You stole because you're greedy."

Emily took a step forward. "I did not. You take that back."

Rachel pointed her finger at Emily. "You're a *thief*, Emily O'Reilly. A criminal. Just like your mother."

The English teacher stepped into the hall and glared at Emily and Rachel. "Girls, move along."

"*She* stopped me, Mrs. Lempinen."

"Doesn't matter." Her frown settled on all the kids lingering in the hall. "All of you, move on."

Emily marched off to class amid the sly glances and whispers with a lump in her throat. There had to be a way to make Rachel tell the truth.

Olivia came alongside Emily. "Don't let her get to you."

"I wish I knew what I'd done to make her hate me so much." She followed Olivia into the hall and toward their lockers. "Enough that she'd lie to the sheriff about me. Did you hear what she said?" She pulled a package of dental floss from her locker and shoved it into her pocket.

Emily and Rachel had been friends, kind of, in elementary school, then all of a sudden, like a switch flipped when they'd entered seventh grade, Rachel had gone out of her way to be mean toward Emily.

"She's just being mean because she's jealous of you." Olivia opened her locker, two down from Emily's.

"Jealous? Of me? How do you figure?" Emily shook her head as she loaded her backpack with the books and folders she'd need for her homework. Olivia must have lost her mind.

"Because Rachel can't stand for anybody to get more attention than her. You always make better grades than her, and you were selected to be on the History Smackdown team and she wasn't."

"Like Rachel cares about an academic challenge team? She's already president of our class and head cheerleader of the junior varsity squad."

Olivia slammed her locker shut. "Emily, have you forgotten who the corporate sponsor for the Smackdown is?"

Oh yeah. Rock Harbor Fishing Resort, owned by Mr. Zinn. Rachel's dad.

Grabbing Emily's backpack and slinging it over her other shoulder, Olivia closed Emily's locker. "You can bet her dad probably wasn't too happy that his darling daughter didn't make the team for the one event his company sponsored."

Emily pressed her lips together. She didn't want to feel sorry for Rachel. Not after the snotty way she'd acted in English class and the way she seemed determined to get her in trouble with the sheriff. But with what Olivia said . . .

"Hey, did you tell your parents that we'd be late coming home from school today?" Olivia asked. "If we hurry, we can make it to the *Kitchigami Journal* office before they close."

"I told Naomi. Let's go." They spilled out of the school with the rest of the kids onto Summit Street, some racing toward the buses while others grabbed their bikes.

Emily and Olivia hurried toward Pepin Street to the local newspaper office.

Rock Harbor's three-block downtown area could have come straight from one of Emily's little brother's picture books. The town's major businesses lined Houghton Street, which was intersected by Jack Pine Lane and Pepin Street. The storefronts were painted in cheerful pastel colors.

Rock Harbor may have been smaller than some towns in the Upper Peninsula, but it more than made up for it with its quirky personality. There were forests on three sides, and Lake Superior stretched out along the other. The Ojibwa called it *Kitchigami*, which meant "giver of life." Emily loved the sound of the surf, but always from a distance. The water scared her silly, and no amount of her friends' teasing could make her get into the water. Ever since she'd nearly drowned, she'd refused to put so much as a toe in. She hated even remembering that day.

"Good, looks like they're still open." Olivia grabbed Emily's hand, and they crossed the street to the newspaper office.

Emily sniffed to see if she could smell the newsprint. "The first newspaper was printed in Boston by Richard Pierce in 1690. And then it was shut down by the administration. Isn't that interesting?"

Olivia gave a little snort. "Not really."

A bell rang as they pushed the door open. Dust floated in the sunlight sneaking in behind them. Emily wrinkled her nose as she let her eyes adjust to the much dimmer light of the newspaper office.

"Hello, young ladies. How may I help you?" Ms. Harris asked, walking in from the back room.

Ms. Harris was tall, with long auburn hair, probably in her forties or so, and wore a business suit. Everyone in town knew she was the newspaper's only reporter.

Emily swallowed. "Um, we need to talk to someone about getting a copy of the paper from about three weeks ago. Please."

"Well, I'm the person who can help you at the moment." The reporter moved toward them, hand extended. "Inetta Harris."

"Yes, ma'am. I've seen you in town, and you were my substitute teacher once when I was in the fifth grade. I'm Emily O'Reilly, and this is my best friend, Olivia Webster."

"Ah, yes. Donovan's little girl. You look like your mother, though."

Emily gave a weak smile. "Naomi's my stepmom."

"I know that. I meant you look like your mother. Your real mother."

"You know my mother?" Emily's voice wavered. It'd been so long since she met someone who actually knew her mother personally.

Ms. Harris chuckled. "Marika and I were friends, right up until she married your dad."

Emily couldn't think straight. It'd been six years since her mother's trial and sentencing. She'd been accused of attempted murder, but had testified against her partner and had gotten a lighter sentence. It'd been years and years since Emily had met someone who knew her mother before all of that.

"You, honey, look exactly like she did as a young woman." Ms. Harris smiled as she patted Emily's hand. "Those beautiful dark curls. Your hair is absolutely gorgeous. And, oh my, you've already got a figure just like Marika's. I was always jealous of her curves."

Heat filled Emily's face. She hated that the top half of her body had grown so much larger than the other girls in her class. She'd begun wearing bigger clothes to keep anyone from noticing.

"Sorry. I know you must miss your mother, and here I am, talking about her when I know she won't even be up for parole for months. Do forgive me." Ms. Harris straightened. "So, what edition of the paper were you interested in, girls?"

*Months?* But Mom had been sentenced to twelve years. It'd only been a little over six. *Breathe.* This couldn't be true, could it? She eyed Ms. Harris's face but decided not to ask.

Olivia took a step forward. "The one that featured the festival with the picture of Mrs. Dancer's jewelry. We'd like a copy of that one, please."

"Ah. Yes." She smiled at Emily again. "I imagine you must be upset. Mary was really not happy with you. I tried to keep the article as neutral as I could." She moved behind the counter. "Let me get your order in." Her fingers flew over a keyboard.

Emily stepped up to the other side of the counter. "What did Mrs. Dancer say about me?"

"It's not what she said, exactly. More like the innuendos."

What did that mean?

Olivia moved beside Emily. "I'm not sure I understand, Ms. Harris."

The lady smiled at Olivia. "By the way Mary kept bringing up Emily's name, even though the sheriff told me there was no physical evidence she'd done anything wrong, I could tell she thought Emily had something to do with the missing necklace."

"But I didn't." Yet everybody in town seemed to think she did. Especially Mrs. Dancer.

"You know, if you could get your dad's permission, I could interview you and run a story of your side of things."

"She can ask them," Olivia butted in. "But for now, we need to hurry and get home. May we please get a copy of that paper?"

Ms. Harris nodded and headed to the back room. "Certainly. Let me grab it for you." She returned in a moment, paper in hand. "That'll be a dollar fifty."

Emily dug in her pocket. She had some change from her lunch money. She pulled out the exact change and handed it to Ms. Harris.

"Thank you, girls."

"Thank you." Emily tucked the paper under her arm and turned behind Olivia. They opened the door, and the bell jingled.

"Don't forget to ask your father about that interview," Ms. Harris called out.

"I will. Thank you." Emily let the door shut behind them before racing with Olivia down the street.

"You aren't really going to ask your father about that interview, are you?" Olivia shifted her backpack on her shoulder.

"Of course not." Emily flattened the newspaper open and

stared at the picture of Mrs. Dancer's Sapphire Beauty. "Wow, it's so beautiful. Even in black and white."

Emily read the article under the picture. She scanned the information about the dates of the upcoming festival, costs, and other exhibitors. She paused when she reached the description of the Sapphire Beauty.

"Listen to this," she told Olivia, then read aloud. "'Legend has it that deep in the forests, there are things that make the bravest of brave shiver. Inhuman things, supernatural things, *savage* things.'" Emily lowered her voice, mimicking the tone her old babysitter had used when she told the tale. "'Strange creatures dwell in the deepest, darkest forests in the world, especially around the Upper Peninsula, but even stranger are the creatures that live *inside* of man, inner beasts more fearsome than anything else.'"

"That's a freaky voice, Em," Olivia said.

"Here's the rest of it." Emily took a breath before finishing. "'During the autumn and winter, it's said the Windigo goes mad with hunger and hunts people. He looks for people lost or alone in the woods. He's hard to kill. Some say he's like a werewolf and must be killed with a silver bullet. Others say you have to burn the body and bury the ashes. One Ojibwa story says a medicine man named Big Goose fought and killed the Windigo with his bare hands.'" Even as she read, Emily's heartbeat kicked up a notch.

Olivia let out a nervous laugh. "No matter how many times you hear the story, it's still creepy."

"The article goes on . . . 'Mrs. Dancer, being a descendant of the Ojibwa tribe, crafted the beautiful Sapphire Beauty, photographed above, to ward off the Windigo. This one-of-a-kind necklace will be for sale at the festival, but it won't come cheap.

This enchanted necklace carries a price tag of over a thousand dollars, a bargain when you see it in person.'"

"Enchanted? That's crazy." Olivia switched her backpack from one shoulder to the other.

"But that's what Mrs. Dancer meant when she said the Windigo would strike while the protection was gone." Emily folded the paper and shoved it into her backpack. "Besides, it got a lot of attention in the paper, which probably made it worth even more to people, I guess."

"And the article told everyone how much it was worth, and when and where they could get their hands on it."

Emily and Olivia started toward Cottage Avenue. Two high school kids stood outside the community center. One of the girls nodded toward Emily, then whispered to her friend. They both snickered, then crossed the street, away from Emily and Olivia.

Emily pressed her lips together. She needed to figure out what really happened to the necklace. Soon. Before her reputation was trashed.

The house was quiet when Emily got home. "Timmy? Naomi?" When no one answered, she went to the kitchen and grabbed apples for herself and Olivia. The phone jingled from the living room. "Olivia, could you grab that?" She held the apples under the faucet, then dried them with a paper towel.

Olivia appeared in the doorway with the portable phone in her hand. She was white, and her eyes were big. She held out the phone. "Em . . ."

Emily frowned and put down the apples before she took the phone. "Hello?"

"Emily. It's so good to hear your voice."

Emily had only heard the woman's voice in her nightmares. Her throat tightened, and she couldn't speak. She shot a panicked glance at Olivia, who mouthed, *I'm sorry.* Swallowing, Emily finally found her voice. "Mom?"

"It's me." Her mother's giggle sounded nervous. "I wanted to hear your voice."

Her heart galloped in her chest. "Does Dad know you are calling?"

"Your father has refused all my calls. I haven't forgotten about you and Timmy, Emily. You kids belong to me and no one else."

"Listen, Mom, I have to go." Emily slammed her finger onto the phone's power button and threw it on the table. All the strength left her legs, and she sank onto a chair. Burying her face in her hands, she let out the sob that had been building.

Olivia knelt beside her. "I'm sorry, Em. The man said he had a collect call from her, and I didn't know what to do. I said yes to accepting the charges just as a reflex. I bet I could have said no."

Emily swallowed hard and tried to get herself under control. "I can't believe she called here. Dad said I didn't have to talk to her ever again and neither did Timmy. She scares me so much." She hugged herself. "She said me and Timmy *belong* to her. What if she gets out and tries to take us?" Her voice rose, and she bit her trembling lip.

"You've got to call your dad."

Emily nodded. Her heartbeat began to slow. "He'll be really mad. She could have killed Timmy! She deliberately tried to make him sick to make it look like Naomi was a bad stepmother. What kind of person would do that to their own kid?"

"I don't know, Em. A sick person, maybe."

Emily rubbed her eyes. "Oh sure, try to make me feel sorry for her. She's just evil, Liv. Some people are."

Olivia nodded. "Your dad will protect you."

"He couldn't protect Timmy. He wanted to, but she was so sneaky."

"He knows how bad she is now. It will be okay. Call your dad." Olivia handed her the phone.

 **FIVE**

"Come on." Timmy was worse than Charley, racing ahead to the field, then bounding back to hurry Emily and Olivia along. "Dave's waiting for us. He said he found out something important."

"We're coming. We're coming." Emily shook her head and grinned at Olivia, but inside, hope burned. Maybe Dave had uncovered something important.

It was hard to be excited about anything when her whole world had just shifted an hour ago. Her dad had been so mad. He'd promised to make sure Mom never called again.

"Hurry up!" Timmy looped back to them again.

"What do you think he found out?" Olivia asked.

Timmy tugged his baseball cap lower on his head. "I don't know. Whatever it is, it had to come from his parents since Dave said Pansy wasn't in school today."

A breeze swept over Rock Harbor, dancing through the higher grass of the field. It carried the scent of the surf that tickled Emily's nose. She shivered as she eyed the forest in the distance. What if there was something to the Windigo legend? She shook her head. No, that was just a story. Right?

"Finally." Timmy bent to rub Samson's head as Dave and the dog joined them. Samson was the star of Kitchigami Search and Rescue. He mostly looked like a German shepherd, but his curly tail was all chow. "I didn't think you were ever going to get here."

"Hey, thanks for calling, Dave." Emily smiled as she approached. "I appreciate all the help I can get."

Together, the four formed a loose circle.

Dave ran his fingers absentmindedly over his dog's head. "I overheard Mom and Dad this afternoon."

While Ranger Kade Matthews wasn't Dave's real dad, he was as good a stepdad to Dave as Naomi was a stepmom to Emily and Timmy. And he'd adopted Dave a couple of years ago, just before the twins were born.

"And?" Emily tried to restrain her impatience.

"Dad told Mom that Mrs. Cooper was back in town."

"How'd your mom react?" Olivia asked.

"What did she say?" Emily added.

"She said she hadn't heard. Dad told her they'd been back for only a couple of weeks, but Mom had been busy with an out-of-town search. Dad said Mrs. Cooper had been looking for jobs, but no one would hire her."

Olivia nodded her head. "Just like my parents said."

"Mom asked where they were staying, and Dad told her that he'd heard she was back in the house she and Mr. Cooper lived in."

Emily bit her lip.

"Dad told her that Mrs. Cooper had been seen selling off pieces of her jewelry at the pawnshops in Marquette."

"What's a pawnshop?" Timmy asked.

"A place where you can sell your valuable stuff and get cash quickly." Dave ducked his head. "At least that's what I heard."

"You're right. It is." Emily's mind raced. If Mrs. Cooper was selling off her jewelry for money, then it made sense she'd steal a valuable necklace and try to pawn it too! "I wonder if Sheriff Kaleva knows that."

"She could have stolen the necklace and pawned it as her own." Olivia's eyes were wide.

Emily nodded. "That's exactly what I was thinking." She turned to Dave. "Did your dad happen to mention the name of the pawnshop?"

He shook his head. "He didn't say, but my mom's planning to go visit Mrs. Cooper."

"When?" Oh, wouldn't she love to listen in on that conversation. Emily knew gossiping and eavesdropping were wrong—Pastor Lukkari preached on the topic every couple of months—but was it okay when she would use the information to clear herself of a crime?

Dave shrugged. "She didn't say."

"Wow. What'd your dad say about that?" Olivia asked.

"He said he didn't think it was the best idea but knew she'd do it anyway."

Olivia and Emily both chuckled. Bree was a take-charge type of woman, one of the reasons Emily wanted to grow up to be just like her.

Dave kept his head ducked. "I feel bad for Pansy. Her dad didn't care if she got hurt. He just did what he wanted."

Timmy knelt down to hug Charley. "Grown-ups sometimes do bad things. My real mom messed up my insulin medication to try and hurt my dad and Naomi. My sugar got all messed up, and I was really sick. It's scary to know that my own mother would try and hurt me to get back at my dad." He buried his face in

Charley's thick fur. "I still get nightmares about her coming back to hurt me."

Emily swallowed back her own emotions. She hadn't told Timmy what Ms. Harris had said about their mother being up for parole in months instead of years. And she sure hadn't told him about her mother's call. Her dad said he would have their number taken off Mom's authorized calling list. Now Emily knew she wouldn't say anything to Timmy. She couldn't. Hopefully, he would never need to know.

She patted her brother's shoulder. "It's okay, Timmy. Dad and Naomi won't ever let her hurt us again."

"I know." Timmy's voice was muffled by Charley's fur.

Samson barked, tail wagging in the air. He whined and looked back the way they'd come just as Dave's cell phone rang.

Dave glanced at the caller ID. "It's my mom. I'd better go. Dinner's probably ready."

"Thanks, Dave. I appreciate it." Emily smiled.

"Sure." He looked at Timmy, who stood. "See you tomorrow at school." Then he opened the cell phone. "Hey, Mom. I'm on my way." He jogged across the field, Samson dogging his heels.

"Charley and I will race you girls home." Timmy took off at a run.

"You know, maybe we shouldn't let the boys help us anymore." Olivia grabbed a piece of grass and twisted it as they walked after Timmy and the dog toward home. "They seemed pretty shook up."

"Yeah, and I didn't realize Timmy still had nightmares."

"Funny how Ms. Harris mentioned your mom."

"Did you catch what she said about my mom's parole? Being in months? I thought it would be another six years." Emily shook her head. "I wonder if Dad and Naomi know." She tried to swallow, but there was a lump in her throat. "I can't believe she called me."

"At least you don't have to talk to her again. And I imagine your dad would have been told if she was up for parole soon. I bet it's just a rumor."

"Yeah." She pushed the worry away. *Months* was still a long way off even if it was true, and she doubted her mother would get paroled. "I wonder how many pawnshops are in Marquette."

"Let's check the Internet and see." Olivia began running after Timmy.

Emily grinned and kicked into running. She easily overtook her best friend and quickly gained on her brother. The wind blew on her face, the scent of home washing over her. The late summer sunshine lifted Emily's spirits. She'd better enjoy it while she could. Once winter hit, the warm sunshine would be replaced by gray clouds.

Much like Emily's happiness would be replaced with sadness if she didn't prove her innocence soon.

It wasn't until after dinner that the girls were able to get onto the Internet without an adult looking over their shoulders.

"Okay, let's see what we have." Emily opened the browser and typed in PAWNSHOP MARQUETTE MICHIGAN. She flexed her fingers as she waited for the page to load. "I hope there aren't many. It would've been easier if Dave had been able to learn the name of which shop Mrs. Cooper had sold the jewelry to."

"There can't be all that many," Olivia whispered. "It's Marquette, only a little bigger than Rock Harbor."

The town's population was about twenty-five hundred, but visitors flooded in during the summer. Tourists came for the fishing and hunting, for the beauty of this land of waterfalls, and for the festivals with their Finnish or Cornish food and fun. Soon the residents would be in the town alone again.

"Oh my gummy bears." Olivia's coarse whisper snapped Emily to the monitor.

Her eyes widened and her hopes dropped to her toes. "Over nine hundred and ninety-two thousand results for pawnshops in Marquette? Seriously?" There was no way she could figure out which one Mrs. Cooper had sold jewelry to.

"Wait a minute. Scroll down. That's just the search engine. A lot of those pages are white and yellow pages listings."

Olivia always had been better with the computer than Emily. "Why don't you do this?" Emily stood and let her best friend take her seat.

"Okay. Let's see." Olivia's pointer rolled the center of the mouse until she came to a page that had a listing in its description. She clicked on the link. "This should tell us how many there really are."

Emily could only hope so.

"Look. If you take out the Goodwill store, the Salvation Army, and the local flea market, that only leaves one pawnshop."

Emily's heart pounded even as she realized Naomi had stopped humming. "Quick, hand me the notebook so I can write down the address."

Olivia passed her the spiral notebook and pen. Emily scribbled the name of the pawnshop, along with the address and phone number, just as the door to Matthew's bedroom clicked shut.

"Exit the Internet," Emily whispered.

Olivia closed the window. They stood as Naomi came down the hall, carrying the latest book she was in the middle of reading.

"What're you girls doing?"

"Research." Emily hugged the notebook to her chest. "But we just finished. I'm about to go brush my teeth and floss."

"Oh, okay. Keep it down. I just got Matthew to sleep."

"Yes, ma'am." Emily led the way to her bedroom and pulled the door behind them.

"That was close," Olivia said as she plopped onto Emily's bed.

"Tell me about it." Emily set the notebook on her desk and joined Olivia on the bed. "But at least we know the pawnshop where Mrs. Cooper sold the jewelry."

"Um, Emily . . . what are you going to do about it? It's not like we can go to Marquette to the pawnshop to see if Mrs. Dancer's necklace is there."

"I don't know yet."

"Maybe we can call the pawnshop and describe the necklace. See if they have it."

Emily chewed her lip. "I don't think they'd give out that information over the phone."

"Maybe we could get someone to take us there."

"Like who?"

Olivia shrugged. "I don't know."

"Wait a minute . . ." The idea came to Emily like a bolt of lightning. "How about we give the tip to Ms. Harris to check out for us? She's a newsperson . . . it'd be natural for her to follow up on a lead."

Olivia sat up straight. "And she seemed to really like you."

Because of her mother. But right now, Emily didn't have any other choice. "Yeah. I bet she'll get right on it."

Emily just wouldn't mention her mother, or parole, or how much she looked like her.

That reminded her that she needed to talk to Timmy and find out about those nightmares. She thought he'd stopped having them years ago. If they were bad, she'd have to tell Naomi and Dad, even if that made Timmy mad at her.

Sometimes doing the right thing was hard.

After brushing their teeth and changing into their pajamas, they climbed into Emily's bed. Within minutes, Olivia's steady breathing told Emily her best friend had fallen asleep.

Emily wasn't so lucky. Her mind raced with so much stuff to think about. Her mom . . . the pawnshop . . .

*Screeeeeccccchhhhh.*

Emily sat upright in bed. What was that sound? Her heart raced. She bit her lip and waited, listening. Nothing.

Letting out a slow breath, she lay back down. With everything going on, it was natural she was hearing things. Olivia would get a kick out of it in the morning when Emily told her. They'd laugh and—

*Screeeeeccccchhhhh.*

That wasn't her imagination! Clutching the covers to her chest, Emily sat up. Her mouth went dry. What *was* that sound? It seemed to be coming from right outside her window. But if that was the case, why wasn't Charley barking up a storm?

The Windigo! It was the Windigo, right outside her window! Did he think she stole the necklace? Was he here to make sure it was never found? Was he going to eat her up?

*Screeeeeccccchhhhh.*

Olivia sat up, rubbed her eyes, and then stared at Emily. "Is that tree rubbing against the house again?" She yawned. "Don't laugh, but it scared me silly last night until I realized what it was."

Emily let out a relieved snort. "Yeah, it's doing it again." She inched back down under the covers.

Olivia rolled over, turning her back to Emily.

*Screeeeeeccccchhhhh.*

Just the tree against the house. Not the Windigo coming for her. Emily exhaled, letting her heart rate slow back down to normal. Just a tree. Not some type of bogeyman. She needed to get a grip. She was too old to believe in such things.

But for a minute there . . . she hadn't been so sure.

What if there really was such a thing as a Windigo?

# SIX

"May we see Ms. Harris, please?" Emily stared at the editor working behind the counter. He stood nearly as tall as her dad, but was much, much thinner. His shoulders stuck out to almost points. His gray hair was thin too. He looked kind of like the picture of Abraham Lincoln in their history book. All he needed was a beard.

"She's covering a story right now." Louis Farmer, editor of the paper, smiled. "May I help you ladies with something?"

Despite his smile, Mr. Farmer didn't look nearly as friendly as Ms. Harris. Emily swallowed. "Um, we're working on a project and needed to talk with her for a few minutes. Do you know where we can find her?"

"Oh, a school project. How fun." His tone was disinterested. He glanced at his watch. "She should be back in a few minutes, if you'd like to wait."

It wasn't exactly a school project, but she'd never said it was. That wasn't really lying, right? Emily looked at Olivia.

"We don't want to be a bother. We'll just wait outside." Olivia moved toward the door.

"Whatever you wish. You're more than welcome to wait inside. She's covering the library's new archival computer system."

"We'll catch up with her, Mr. Farmer." Emily opened the door. "Thank you."

They left the *Kitchigami Journal* office and headed to the library. If Ms. Harris was finished with her story, they'd pass her. As they walked, folks raking leaves and mulching flower beds stopped to wave or say hello. Everyone seemed to be outside, enjoying the last weeks of summer before snow took over the Upper Peninsula.

"Shouldn't you be in prison for stealing or something?"

Emily and Olivia stopped to turn at the corner of Houghton and Jack Pine. Emily spun, facing Rachel Zinn, who stood outside the Coffee Place with her circle of friends. Gretchen wasn't with her.

Rachel's nose was in the air. "You stole Mary Dancer's necklace, and you should be in jail, just like your mom. Maybe you two could bunk together."

Her entire body stiff, Emily couldn't even speak. Her throat was tight. Was that what everyone in town thought?

"Why are you so mean, Rachel?" Olivia hollered out. "She didn't steal any necklace."

Rachel huffed. "Of course you'd take up for her. She's your best friend. But I heard her, and so did Gretchen."

Emily found her voice. "I never said I was going to take Mrs. Dancer's necklace." She curled her hands into fists at her sides.

"Yes, you did." Rachel giggled as one of her friends leaned over and whispered something in her ear. "Guess it runs in the family, huh? You and your mom. Is your little brother a criminal too, or is it only the women in your family who belong behind bars?"

Olivia grabbed Emily's arm. "I don't know what you think you heard, Rachel, but she never said she planned to take Mrs. Dancer's necklace."

Rachel just laughed. Emily took a step toward the street, her heart pumping blood so fast that her ears rang. *Say something.* Her throat was tight, and her eyes burned.

Olivia held tight to Emily's arm. "Just let it go. It's not even worth it." She tossed a glare at the laughing girls. "*She's* not worth it."

She had to tug hard on Emily before Emily allowed Olivia to lead her down Jack Pine Street. Emily didn't want to leave while the girls were laughing. "I can't believe she brought Mom into this. And Timmy! How dare she?"

Olivia shook her head as she stopped on the sidewalk to stare at Emily. "I don't know what's wrong with her, but we should ignore her."

Emily's throat was still tight. "That's easy for you to say. She's not picking on you and your family."

"I'm sorry." Olivia gave her a hug. "Come on, let's go see Ms. Harris. If we can clear your name, then Rachel will be proven wrong."

"And she'd better be doing some serious apologizing."

But even an apology wouldn't stop the town from talking about her mother. Emily lifted her head high and did her best not to cry. She'd show them she was *not* like her mother. Finally, they reached their destination and left Rachel and her clique behind.

"Why, hello, girls."

They stopped and turned to find Ms. Harris exiting the side door. "What perfect timing to see you again so soon."

"We were looking for you," Emily said.

"Really?" Ms. Harris's eyebrows rose as she smiled. "Your father will let you do the interview?"

"No. Well, he hasn't said yet." Emily hadn't exactly asked him, but that was beside the point. "But I do think I have a story for you, Ms. Harris." Although Emily was having second thoughts. It was like accusing someone of stealing with no proof. Just like Emily felt Mrs. Dancer had accused her.

"Please, call me Inetta. When you say Ms. Harris, I feel really old." She waggled her eyebrows and grinned. "Why don't we grab a pastry at the Suomi Café? I could use a little snack since I skipped lunch today."

Emily looked at Olivia, who shrugged. "Sure, I guess."

They walked along Houghton Street, a gentle breeze dancing leaves along the street. "Did you know the library just received the latest technological archiving system? The grant request was finally approved. It's a nice setup. I'm impressed."

Emily nodded. It'd been a long time since she'd been in the library.

They reached the café and stepped inside. The aroma of Finnish cardamom bread filled the Suomi Café as they entered. The worn plank floors of the restaurant and the cracked leather booths showed the place was well loved and well used. Emily caught a glimpse of a *panukakkua*, a custard pancake drizzled with hot raspberry syrup, on the passing waitress's tray. Her stomach growled in response.

"Let's grab a seat here." Inetta pulled out a chair at a corner table and motioned for the girls to do the same.

The waitress came immediately. Inetta ordered a cup of coffee and a *pulla*, a Finnish sweet roll, for herself, then looked at Emily. "What would you girls like?"

"Oh, nothing." Probably a good thing she'd left her savings at home. She'd spend every dime she had on *panukakkua*.

"I'd like a glass of water, please," Olivia said.

"You can't let me sit here and eat something all by myself. You simply must have something. My treat." Inetta smiled at the waitress. "Sweet things, they don't want to ruin their dinners." She darted her gaze between Emily and Olivia. "How about you girls split something?"

"We'll share a *panukakkua*," Emily blurted out. Her taste buds were already dancing. "And I'll have a water too."

"You can't have water with such a delicious pastry. How about a mocha?" Inetta asked.

Emily nodded.

Inetta smiled at the waitress. "And two mochas, please."

The waitress hurried away but returned within moments to set steaming coffee drinks in front of them, then rushed off again. Emily could only hope the lady didn't mention her being in the café to Dad or Naomi. This could be a little difficult to explain.

"So"—Inetta stirred a packet of sweetener into her coffee— "what's this *maybe* story you have for me?"

Emily looked at Olivia. Maybe this was a bad idea. It felt wrong to accuse Mrs. Cooper without any proof. But how was she going to find out if Mrs. Dancer's necklace had been sold to the pawnshop if she didn't tell Inetta?

"We heard there's a possibility that Mrs. Dancer's missing necklace might have been sold at this pawnshop in Marquette." Olivia handed the slip of paper with the name, address, and phone number on it to Inetta.

That was perfect. No names, no accusations. Emily smiled at her clever best friend.

Inetta read the paper. "Are you sure about this?"

Emily shrugged. "We can't be positive."

"Because you can't go to Marquette to check it out."

"Right." Olivia nodded.

The waitress chose that moment to return to the table with the Finnish pastries. She set them on the table, refilled Inetta's coffee, then disappeared behind the counter.

Emily's mouth watered as she used the fork to cut the *panukakkua* in half. The custard pancake steamed, and the hot raspberry sauce drizzled to the plate. The delicate pastry was light as Emily stuck a bite into her mouth. Her taste buds sang as she closed her eyes and savored.

Inetta laughed. "I'm glad you decided to have something after all."

Heat spread across Emily's cheeks, but Olivia's and Inetta's grins made her smile too. "I love these."

"We can tell." Olivia giggled.

"Now, about this pawnshop?"

Emily swallowed, then took a sip of her drink. "Yes, you're right. We don't know that the necklace is at that shop, but we suspect it might be."

"Interesting." Inetta took a bite of her *pulla*, chewing slowly. "Why would you think the necklace might be there?"

Emily's face flushed with heat again. She took another sip of her mocha to wash down the bite she'd just swallowed. How could she tell Inetta enough without accusing Mrs. Cooper or getting Dave in trouble?

Olivia wiped her mouth and then wadded her paper napkin into a ball. She set it on the table in front of her. "We overheard someone say that some jewelry from Rock Harbor had been sold there recently."

"Eavesdropping?" Inetta asked.

"More like someone told someone who told someone else who told us." Olivia finished her mocha.

"Ah. You don't want to tell me." Inetta laid her fork across her empty plate.

The waitress returned with the check. Inetta thanked her. She tossed a couple of bills on the table, then stood. Olivia and Emily followed her as she wove through the restaurant and stepped out onto the street.

Emily cleared her throat. "I just know what it's like to be accused of something you didn't do."

Inetta stopped at the intersection. "How about I go to this pawnshop and see if the necklace is there? If it is, I'll call Sheriff Kaleva and he can do his job. If it's not, I'll question the pawn-shop owner to see if anyone tried to sell it. I'll let you girls know what he says. How's that sound?"

"Perfect." Emily grinned so wide her face hurt. "Thank you, Inetta."

"I know you want to clear your name, Emily. I'll help as I can, but know that I can only go so far on your theories." Inetta smiled gently. "I hope you'll learn to trust me. There will come a point and time when you'll have to tell me more than you really want to. Please remember I'm a journalist, which means I protect my sources. I won't say anything unless you tell me I can. Okay?"

Emily nodded. So did Olivia.

"Okay then." Inetta let out a long breath. "I'll have time to run over to Marquette tomorrow before lunch. Why don't we meet back here tomorrow afternoon, about the same time as today?"

"Sure," Emily said.

"I'll see you tomorrow, then." Inetta headed toward the news-paper office.

The girls crossed the intersection and walked to Cottage Avenue. Rock Harbor's streets were packed with people strolling around, a sign of late summer's high traffic. Flyers about the big surfing championship filled every storefront window.

Emily paused as she read one of the advertisements. "Malia Spencer's still in town?"

"Yeah. I heard her tell the surf team that she'd be here for the next two weeks until the championship. She'll be giving demonstrations there." Olivia stared at Emily. "Why? What are you thinking?"

"Well, she was at the festival. Remember, we saw her?"

"So? Just about everybody in Rock Harbor was at the festival."

"But we saw her. From our booth."

Olivia shook her head. "Are you saying Malia Spencer, famous Hawaiian surfer who probably has more money than she knows what to do with, stole Mrs. Dancer's necklace?" She chuckled.

"Well, put like that . . ." It did sound silly. But someone had to have taken the necklace.

Grabbing her hand, Olivia tugged her toward the O'Reilly home. "Come on, forget about Malia as a suspect."

Emily fell into step with her best friend. "You're right."

Olivia slowed as they reached the end of the driveway. "You know, just about everybody in Rock Harbor will be at the championship too."

"Yeah?"

"Well, what better place to nose around to see if there's anything new about the missing necklace?"

"That's in a couple of weeks, Olivia."

"So?"

Emily shook her head. "That's too close to my birthday. I want to find out who really took the necklace before then. Otherwise, I won't get my puppy!" Saying it out loud made it feel too real. Tears burned her eyes.

Olivia gave her a sideways hug. "Maybe Inetta will find the necklace tomorrow, and this will all be over for you."

"I hope so." Emily led the way through the back door into the house.

Because she had to have this mess all cleared up before her birthday.

She just *had* to get her puppy!

 **SEVEN**

"Yeah, it's cool. We got new team wet suits and board bags and leashes." Josh's blue eyes sparkled.

Emily stood on the outskirts of Josh's group hovering by the student bulletin board in the hall, hanging on his every word.

"I thought you said the team was hard up for funds." Brandon, the captain of the team, shoved Josh's shoulder in a playful way. "Have you been holding out on us?"

"Nah, man. These were courtesy of a donor."

"A donor? Who could afford all that?" Brandon asked.

"Don't know. Anonymous." Josh shrugged. "Who cares? We needed the stuff. I'm just glad we got everything before the championship."

An anonymous donor dropping down hundreds of dollars? Emily pressed her lips together and leaned in closer.

"Yeah, whatever." Brandon clapped Josh's shoulder. "We gonna win this year?"

"You know it." Josh turned and pinned something on the bulletin board.

"What's that?"

"Just a call-out for team helper volunteers. I promised Coach I'd put it up for him. Let's go." Josh led the group down the hall and out of the school.

Emily stared after him. As far as she knew, no school team had ever gotten a large donation from an anonymous donor. Money was tight for all families right now. At least, that's what Dad said when he and Naomi discussed the hardware store business. Who would have money to give away as a donation? Seemed a little suspicious, considering the surf team had hosted several fund-raisers over the last couple of months. If someone had wanted to make such a donation, wouldn't they have done so before now?

"What are *you* doing hanging around here, thief?"

Emily spun around. She'd had enough. "What's your problem, Rachel?"

Rachel's eyes widened. "I'm fine, Emily. It's you who is the problem. Everyone knows you stole Mary Dancer's necklace. You're a thief, and probably a cheater too. Maybe that's why you get such good grades. And maybe you cheated your way onto the History Smackdown team."

"I'm not a cheater, and I'm no thief." Emily took a step toward Rachel.

Mrs. Moon, the algebra teacher, moved in their direction. "Is there a problem here, girls?"

Rachel smiled her fake, sweet smile at the teacher. "No, ma'am."

"Then move along." Mrs. Moon crossed her arms over her chest and monitored the hall's traffic flow.

Rachel tossed Emily a final sneer, then bounced off with her friends.

"Hey, I waited for you at the locker." Olivia stepped beside

Emily and nodded toward Rachel's back. "Was she starting trouble again?"

"Doesn't she always?"

"Don't let her get to you." Olivia smiled. "Why are you here, anyway? Her locker is just down the row."

"I came over for this." Emily pointed at the bulletin board. "Did you know an anonymous donor gave the surf team new wet suits and board bags?"

"No. And I should care about this, why?"

Emily filled Olivia in on what she'd overheard from Josh. "I just think that's really coincidental, don't you?"

Olivia shrugged. "Could be. But there's no way you can find out who the donor is. Especially since you aren't even on the surf team."

Emily glanced at the bulletin board. "I could be one of the team helper volunteers, though." Olivia would see through her in half a second.

"Are you serious?" Olivia's hazel eyes went wide. "You can't even swim."

Pointing at the sheet Josh had posted, Emily said, "I don't think swimming is part of the job. Helping keep track of the team equipment and stuff is what they do."

Olivia laughed. "Yeah, right. You can't even stand to be too close to the water, Em."

True, but the posting said nothing about getting in the water. "I'm going to talk to the coach."

"You're serious?"

"I am." Emily let out a sigh. "It's the only way I might be able to learn something about this donor."

"You just want to be close to Josh."

Heat burned Emily's face. "Well, that's a bonus, yeah, but you know it's not the main reason I'm going to do this."

"I know. I was just teasing you." Olivia handed Emily her backpack. "I grabbed your stuff for you."

"Thanks. You going to come with me to the coach's office?"

"Sure. Do you really think I'd let you sign up by yourself? Someone's gotta keep an eye on you."

Emily smiled and headed toward the gym under the covered walkway. The wind had picked up, and the crash of the waves from Lake Superior washed over the little town. Emily shivered despite the seventy-degree temperature.

Sneakers squeaked on the basketball court as Emily and Olivia made their way to the coach's office in the back part of the gymnasium. The door sat ajar, and the coach was on the phone with his back to the door.

"I understand that, and we appreciate everything we get, but right now we really need a couple more backup boards. If one of our team's boards breaks, we'll be disqualified." The coach tossed a pencil onto his desk.

Emily chewed her bottom lip. It sure didn't sound like the team was rolling in money.

The coach hunched in his chair. "Then do whatever you have to do to get another donor on the line. We *will* take the championship this year." His voice sounded harsh. Cold. Mean.

Olivia stared at Emily, who stared right back. Who was he talking to?

"See that you do." The coach slammed the phone down.

Emily quickly knocked on the cracked door. "Hello? Coach Larson?" Maybe the coach wouldn't realize they'd been eavesdropping.

"Yes?" He swiveled in his chair and pierced her with a scowl. He was a big guy with fair, thinning hair and a thin Finnish nose.

"I'm here to sign up to be a surf team helper volunteer." She smiled as widely as she could.

"A what?" His thoughts were clearly still on the disturbing phone call.

"I saw a notice on the bulletin board. Josh put it up there?"

"Oh. Yeah." He stared at them. "So you want to be helpers, eh?"

She forced herself to stand tall and smile. "Yes, sir."

"Okay. Let me get you the permission slips." He opened a desk drawer and rummaged through papers. "You'll have to come to all the practices and, of course, the competitions." He opened another desk and continued rummaging. "Where did I put those things?" He slammed another drawer. "Oh, here they are." He handed two slips to them. "Fill these out, have a parent sign, then bring them back to me, and we'll get you signed up."

Emily took them. "Thank you."

The coach met her eye and gave a curt nod, clearly dismissing them.

She motioned to Olivia, and they left.

"Wow, that was intense. I'm almost glad I can't sign up yet." Olivia hustled down the walkway toward the street.

Emily stopped dead in her tracks. "Why not?" It was one thing to be brave in word, but totally different in deed.

Olivia nodded to the slips in Emily's hand. "I can't exactly get a parent's signature, now, can I? Not until my parents get back from their cruise."

Rats! Olivia had a point. "But will you? I mean, after your parents get back?" That would still let her help out for the big competition.

"Sure." Olivia stopped walking and tilted her head. "Are you kind of not sure about this, Em? You don't have to do it. I know how much water scares you."

"No, I just wanted an extra pair of ears." Which was true, but not the entire truth. Olivia gave her courage. With her friend there, the water wouldn't be so scary. But now wasn't the time to admit her fear. "We'd better hurry or Inetta will think we forgot about her."

They reached the street and turned toward the Suomi Café, walking faster. The gong of the fog bell out in Lake Superior rang, its echoes filling the streets of Rock Harbor. Goose bumps pricked Emily's arm, and she had no idea why. She shook it off and quickened her pace.

They spotted Inetta as soon as they entered the café and rushed to join her at a corner table. Already waiting on them were a *panukakkua* and two steaming mochas.

"You didn't have to order us this, Inetta, but thank you."

"I don't like eating alone." Inetta chuckled. "So, how was school today?"

"It was okay."

Olivia plopped her backpack to the floor for emphasis. "This early in the year it ought to be illegal to give so much homework."

Inetta shook her head. "But enjoy school while you can. All too soon you grow up and have to face the real world." Her expression turned almost sad. "Growing up isn't all it's cracked up to be. Sometimes it's hard." She gave a little shake, then smiled at Emily. "So let me tell you about my trip to the pawnshop today."

Emily slipped a bite of the Finnish pastry into her mouth while Olivia took a sip of her mocha.

"I met with the owner. Really nice man. He was more than happy to share information with me."

Emily swallowed and took a sip of mocha.

"Did you find the necklace?" Olivia asked.

Inetta smiled. "No. I'm sorry to say it wasn't there. And the owner hadn't seen it. I gave him a copy of the picture we took for the article."

Emily slouched in her seat. She had really been hoping the necklace would be at the pawnshop.

"But he's going to keep an eye out for it and promised to call if he saw it." Inetta ran her finger along the rim of her nearly empty coffee cup. "He did tell me that someone had been selling some jewelry recently, though. Really nice, high-dollar jewelry. Like diamond brooches and earrings."

Inetta finished off the last bite of her *pulla*. "He said he checked all the reports and these items weren't reported stolen, but he showed me some of the pieces—they're nice. Much better than the stuff he usually gets in the shop. I took pictures and am going to do some research."

Emily's mouth went dry. "Why would you research that?" She shrugged and pushed her fork around the plate. "I mean, there's nothing illegal about selling your jewelry, is there?"

"No, but even though it wasn't reported stolen, I'm suspicious. He said the woman who sold them looked nervous."

Olivia cleared her throat. "Or maybe she was emotional about having to sell her jewelry."

Inetta looked from Emily to Olivia. "Okay, girls, what's going on? I have a feeling you know about these pieces of jewelry." She snapped her fingers. "Wait a minute . . . The reason you believed

Mary Dancer's necklace might have been sold to the pawnshop . . . You know who sold this jewelry, don't you?"

Emily fidgeted in her seat. "We don't know for sure, but we have a good idea."

Inetta stared at Emily, then Olivia. Then she sighed. "And you girls don't trust me enough yet to tell me about it, right?"

"It's not that, it's really not," said Olivia. "It's just that if this person is selling off her jewelry, it's because she has no other choice."

"But you thought maybe she'd stolen Mary Dancer's necklace and sold it?"

"Well, not necessarily," Emily began. "She could have been selling it for Mrs. Dancer."

"Which means you think Mary lied about the necklace being missing?" Inetta shook her head. "It's okay for now. I'll take you girls at your word that you think this person is legitimately selling her own jewelry."

"We're pretty certain she is." Olivia nodded.

Throwing several bills onto the table, Inetta stood and slung her purse strap over her shoulder. "Tell you what . . . if I get any leads about the necklace, I'll let you know. And if you girls get another lead or even an idea, you let me know so I can follow up on it. Deal?"

Emily pushed to her feet. "Yes, ma'am."

"Good." Inetta glanced at her watch. "Now, I have to get back to work or Mr. Farmer will wonder what happened to me. You girls stay out of trouble and come see me."

"Yes, ma'am," Olivia said as she grabbed her backpack from the floor.

"Thanks, Inetta. For everything." Emily extended her hand.

Inetta smiled, then shook Emily's hand. "Thank you. See you later."

Emily waited until the reporter had left to take her last sip of mocha and grab her backpack. "Well, that was a dead end."

Out on the curb, Olivia waited for Emily to situate her backpack. "Maybe you'll find out something with the surf club."

"Yeah." But Emily wasn't going to hold her breath. She marched toward the road home.

"Aw, come on, Em . . . we'll get a lead." Olivia followed her.

"From where?" She kicked a rock down the sidewalk. "And what's the sheriff doing? Nothing. I haven't seen him doing any investigating on the case at all. It's like he's accepted that I was the one who took Mrs. Dancer's necklace, based on nothing more than Rachel Zinn's lies."

"If that's true, then why hasn't he arrested you?" Olivia asked.

This wasn't going as planned. Not at all. She saw how the kids looked at her at school. Even her family was acting differently. And it wasn't fair when she hadn't done anything wrong. "Maybe he's waiting on Dad and Naomi to wear me down so he can swoop in and recover the necklace and look like a hero."

"You know he's not doing that." Olivia caught up and fell into step with her. "You probably just haven't seen the work he's doing. I'm sure he's working on the case. Hey, he might even have a lead."

"Then he would have told Dad or Naomi." Emily stopped and faced her best friend. "Do you always believe the best in everyone all the time?"

Olivia laughed. "Emily O'Reilly, you've been my best friend for how many years? You should know the answer to that."

Despite herself, Emily giggled. "Yeah, you do." She reached out and hugged Olivia. "It's one of the things I love most about you."

Olivia squeezed her back. "Cheer up. I've been praying we get a lead."

"I hope God hears you." It seemed he hadn't heard her pleas yet. Or he'd said no. Emily straightened and adjusted the backpack. She glanced over Olivia's shoulder toward the Coffee Place. Thank goodness Rachel and her followers weren't there again.

Bree opened the door of the popular coffee shop. Emily grabbed Olivia's hand. "Come on."

"What? We just had a snack."

"Look." Emily tugged her across the street and moved her to the side. People moved up and down the sidewalk, Rock Harbor residents and tourists alike.

"Oh-kay. Bree is getting coffee. She's always getting coffee."

Emily nodded slowly. "And who's sitting at the table by the cashier?"

"That's . . ." Olivia leaned closer and squinted around the busy coffee shop. "Oh. That's Mrs. Cooper."

"Yep. Let's go use the ladies' room. I don't think we can chance missing what's going on between them. Besides, I need to floss."

And who knew? She just might find out something useful.

 **EIGHT**

"Shh." Emily led Olivia around the mass of people to the table behind where Mrs. Cooper sat.

"I wonder where Pansy is," Olivia whispered.

"Don't know." Emily tilted her head toward the line.

Olivia wore a worried expression. "We're sneaking around to spy. This is really wrong, Emily."

"No, we're trying to get information to clear my name. That's not wrong."

"How does spying on this meeting help clear your name?"

"Shh, Bree is almost to the cashier. She's bound to see Mrs. Cooper any minute now." She moved out of Bree's line of sight and pulled Olivia with her.

Bree chatted with the cashier while she paid for her cappuccino, then turned. Emily had the perfect vantage point to see Bree's face as her gaze landed on Mrs. Cooper. Emily held her breath for the five seconds it took for a range of expressions to cross Bree's face, but mostly surprise.

On the sixth second, Bree stepped beside Mrs. Cooper's table. "Hello, Lucy."

Emily couldn't see Mrs. Cooper's face since her back was to them, but she had no problem hearing the surprise in her voice. "H-hello, Bree."

Bree cleared her throat. "May I sit with you for a moment?"

"S-s-sure." The hesitation in her voice tugged against Emily's conscience. She'd all but accused the woman of stealing and pawning Mrs. Dancer's necklace. With not a single bit of proof except that Mrs. Dancer had shown it to her.

"How is Pansy? She must have grown so much." Bree's cheeks had little red spots on them as she slipped into the chair.

"She's adjusting to being back in town. Being in school. Back in the house."

Bree gave a soft smile. "I imagine it's difficult at times."

Mrs. Cooper nodded. "Bree, I know what people think—that I knew what he was doing."

"Shh." Bree laid her hand over Mrs. Cooper's. "You had nothing to do with any of that. We all know that."

Mrs. Cooper's shoulders shook like she was crying. "Sure doesn't feel that way." She sniffed. "The way everybody in town is treating me." She sniffed again.

Bree handed her a napkin. "What's going on?"

Mrs. Cooper dabbed her face with the napkin, then blew her nose. "I thought coming home would be just that, coming home. But everyone's avoiding me. Like I knew anything about what Pete was doing. I didn't. I promise you, Bree, I had no idea. All that money . . ."

"I know. I believe you."

"No one will give me a job. Not even a chance."

Emily recognized the expression on Bree's face. It said she'd made up her mind to do something about a problem.

"It just so happens that we're looking i
Kitchigami Search-and-Rescue Training C
interested?"

Mrs. Cooper's head came up. "Bree, you do
up a job to give me."

"Seriously. I've had someone filling in, but she's go
lined up in Houghton. She starts October first, so if yo
start tomorrow, she'd have plenty of time to train you befo
leaves. That would be perfect."

"You don't have to give me the job, Bree. I'm sure there are
more qualified people."

"I know you'd be good at this." Bree smiled. "And I'd love to
spend more time with you. I've missed you." Her voice was soft.

Mrs. Cooper pressed her trembling lips together and inhaled.
"Okay. I'll take it. What time tomorrow?"

Bree smiled wider. "How about eight?"

Emily grabbed Olivia's hand and led her out of the Coffee
Place, making sure she kept their backs to Bree and Mrs. Cooper
until they spilled out onto the street.

"Well, that wasn't useful." Olivia straightened her backpack
as they headed to Emily's. "I feel like we just eavesdropped with
no real reason."

"It was useful. We know Mrs. Cooper didn't sell the necklace
at the pawnshop, and she would've while she was there, if she'd
had it."

Olivia shook her head as they turned the corner. "We knew
all that before we stepped foot inside the Coffee Place."

"But now we know that she's got a job, so we can call Timmy
and Dave off their task of getting close to Pansy, although I do feel
sorry for her, so I want Timmy to keep an eye out for her. People

head of Olivia so her best

why she wanted to hear

t she did. Naomi *was*

 girl. Was that always

on our list."

ooper was a good

...e necklace." Poor

...ecause of her father's theft.

...ciate to that feeling a little *too* much.

...u. Olivia waited for a car to pass before they crossed

the street. "But I think I'll feel that way about anybody in Rock Harbor."

"Yeah. Ditto." They headed toward Emily's house.

Olivia stepped onto the sidewalk. "Maybe the person who took the necklace isn't from Rock Harbor."

"Maybe." But that meant they weren't even on the right track in their investigation.

The afternoon carried a hint of a chilly breeze as they walked toward home. If the thief was just a tourist, Emily's chance to find the necklace and clear her name would be gone before the first freeze of the season.

Olivia stopped and stared. "Hey, whose truck is that in the driveway?"

Emily peered past her. She didn't recognize the pickup parked beside Grandma's car under the tree beside the driveway. "I don't know. Let's find out." She hurried the rest of the way to the front door. "Dad? Naomi?"

"In here."

She tossed her backpack onto the bench in the entryway. Olivia did the same before following Emily into the den.

A shaggy-haired man who had freckles almost exactly like Naomi's sat on the couch beside Grandma. A red-haired woman sat on the other side of him, her hand holding his.

"Uncle Greg came to visit." Timmy bounced up as soon as Emily and Olivia entered.

Naomi smiled from her perch on the arm of Dad's chair. "Emily, do you remember my brother, Greg? He was in our wedding? And, Greg, meet Emily's best friend, Olivia Webster." Naomi smiled at Emily and Olivia. "This is his friend, Valerie Syers. She's been in town for a couple of weeks."

Uncle Greg grinned. "Might be hard to remember me. The wedding seems like a long time ago." He offered his hand to Olivia. "Not only am I Naomi's brother, but your dad here was, and still is, one of my best friends ever. We were almost inseparable when we were your age."

Olivia shook his hand while Dad laughed. "Yes, we were, Greg. Those were the good ole days."

Olivia took a seat on the lounging chaise beside Timmy, but her eyes locked onto Emily's and screamed she had something she was dying to tell Emily.

"I completely forgot you had a brother." Emily realized how rude that sounded and clamped a hand over her mouth as she stared at Naomi.

Naomi blushed while Greg chuckled. "Let's just say that for a while, I wasn't the best brother in the world."

"Not like me. I'm the best brother." Timmy jumped up again and danced around the room, Charley nipping at his heels.

Emily laughed. "Yeah. Sure. Right."

Greg, Dad, and Grandma all chuckled while Naomi just got redder in the face.

"Anyway, Greg's going to be staying in Rock Harbor for a few weeks," Dad said.

"Greg—er, Uncle Greg, will you be staying here with us?" The only other adult-sized bed was Emily's, and the house was already a little cramped with Olivia.

Grandma smiled. "Of course not, dear. He'll be staying with me at the bed-and-breakfast." She patted Greg's leg. "I've missed having my son around. This will give him the chance to see how enjoyable the B&B is to manage. How profitable."

Greg's face turned almost as red as Naomi's. "Mom, I already told you, I'm not interested in the place. Too confining. Too stifling."

Grandma's face fell, then brightened again. "I think you've forgotten how lovely Rock Harbor is. If you stay for a little while, I bet you won't find it confining or stifling."

Emily glanced over at Olivia, who widened her eyes, then jerked her gaze to the woman beside Greg—Valerie, was it?— then back to Emily and then widened her eyes even more. What? She didn't know the woman, couldn't see what Olivia's deal was. Valerie was beautiful. Maybe that was it. Maybe she was a famous model. Olivia wanted to be a model when she grew up, so she was always reading those fashion magazines and talking about designers and stuff. That was probably it. Emily smiled at Olivia and nodded.

"So, Greg," Dad interrupted, "what have you been doing with yourself? Last we heard, you were doing some photography work."

"Well, that didn't pan out. So I've been doing a little of this, a little of that in the meantime." He grinned and winked at Timmy.

"Well, if you put down roots, you could settle down. Stay out of trouble for good." Grandma straightened her back.

Emily had never felt such tension. Well, except when Dad and Naomi talked about her mother when they thought Emily couldn't hear.

"Mom, let him breathe. He just got to town today." Naomi stood. "I'm going to wake Matthew from his nap." She headed down the hallway.

Grandma shifted to see over Greg to Valerie. "Valerie, dear, what do you do?"

"Me?" Valerie laid her hand over her chest. "I'm a model."

Greg threw his arm around Valerie's shoulders. "Not just any model. She's the new face for Surf's Up bathing suit line."

"I have several photo shoots set during the championship." Valerie tossed her red hair over her shoulder.

Emily looked at Olivia and grinned. *Ha.* She'd caught that one. Olivia should be proud. But her best friend didn't look proud. She looked like she had a secret that was ready to erupt. Emily stood. "Dad, can we go work on some jewelry before dinner."

"Sure, go ahead. Our guests are staying for dinner, so you might need to help Naomi in a bit anyway."

They'd barely made it into Emily's room and shut the door before Olivia exploded. "Did you recognize her?"

"Valerie? As a model?" Emily set her backpack on the floor beside Olivia's. "Not at first, but you know I'm not as into the whole fashion thing like you."

"That's not what I'm talking about. It's her."

Emily sank to the bed while Olivia paced. "Her who?" She grabbed her *Phantom of the Opera* throw pillow and pulled it against her chest.

Olivia sighed from behind clenched teeth. "The woman part of the couple."

"I'm sorry, Liv, I have no idea what you're talking about."

Bouncing down onto the bed beside Emily, Olivia said, "The couple at the festival—who bought something from Mrs. Dancer's booth during the time the necklace went missing. Valerie is the woman."

"*That* woman?" This could be huge. Emily closed her eyes and went back to that day. Malia Spencer across the street . . . the man clearing his throat . . . she rushed to Mrs. Dancer's table and sold the green fused glass necklace the woman held. Yes, it was Valerie.

Emily opened her eyes and tossed her pillow aside. She grabbed her notebook, then flipped it open to the page of her suspects. She scratched out *The Couple* and wrote *Valerie Syers* out beside it. "Who was the man Valerie was with at the festival? Can you remember what he looked like?"

"He was older than Valerie. I remember he had a lot of gray hair. More than either of our dads have." Olivia shrugged. "He was about the same height as her. I don't remember him being taller, do you?"

Emily shook her head. "Maybe her father?"

"He wasn't that much older."

"A brother?"

Olivia scrunched her nose. "I didn't get that impression. I actually thought they were together. You know, together-together."

"But she and Uncle Greg look like they're together-together." Oh, this was complicated. "Hey, don't models have bodyguards or something with them?"

"I don't know. Some do, I guess. He didn't look bulky enough to be a bodyguard, though." Olivia crossed her arms over her chest. "How can we find out who he is, and who he is to her?"

Emily chewed the end of her pencil. "Maybe we could just ask her?"

"Right. 'Hi, Valerie, we saw you at the festival this past weekend, and you were with a man you seemed chummy with. Who is he?'" Olivia shook her head. "I don't see that happening. If she's with-with your uncle, I don't think she'd say she was dating someone else if that's the truth."

Good point. But there had to be something . . . "The necklace!"

"What about it?"

"If she's wearing the necklace she bought of Mrs. Dancer's, we can ask her about it and maybe figure out a way to work in who she was with."

"Good idea." Olivia frowned. "But what if she isn't wearing it?"

Hmm. "Well, if she has on any jewelry, maybe I can figure out a way to bring up my jewelry, which will open the door to talk about the festival."

"I guess it's worth a try."

Emily shut the notebook. At least it was something. "I think I'll work on my jewelry. Grandma said she'd display some necklaces for me." She began to pull out the boxes of beads. "I don't feel like working on them, though."

Olivia joined her. "Me neither. But you need to earn money for that puppy."

 **NINE**

"Amen." Emily lifted her head from the prayer and elbowed Olivia.

Everyone passed bowls around the table, each spooning food onto their plate. The dining room smelled of onion from the stew Naomi had made. Emily's mouth watered as she filled her bowl before passing it on to Olivia. She grabbed a semmel roll, steaming from the oven. She slathered butter across the middle—it melted immediately on the soft, yeasty bread.

Emily waited until conversations started around the table to check out Valerie's neck. Okay, mainly she waited until Dad and Naomi were engrossed in a conversation with Uncle Greg. She had to lean almost as if whispering to Grandma to see around Valerie's collar. Disappointment burned her throat when she spied only a dainty gold chain.

"Are you okay, dear?" Grandma asked.

Busted. "Uh." Emily glanced at the brooch pinned on Grandma's blouse. "I was just admiring your pin. It's lovely."

Grandma beamed. "Why, thank you, dear. Greg and Naomi's father gave it to me many, many years ago."

Emily looked at Valerie, who had turned to listen in. Here was an opportunity. Emily pushed on. "Don't you think the brooch is lovely, Valerie?"

The model nodded. "It's exquisite." She peered closer. "Ivory?"

"Did you know that George Washington's false teeth were made from ivory? Well, and human and cow teeth too," Emily said.

The model's smile became a grimace. Dad and Greg continued telling stories of their youth, making Naomi chuckle in between Matthew's stunts for attention, completely ignoring the conversation at the other end of the dining table.

"Why, I do believe it *is* ivory." Grandma smiled.

Emily recognized an opening when she saw it. Especially since Dad and Naomi were still otherwise occupied. "Valerie, as a model, I bet you know a lot about jewelry."

"Oh, I suppose every girl takes an interest in jewelry." She smiled a little too wide at Emily, and included Olivia as well. "Don't you, girls?"

"I certainly do," Olivia said, "but nothing like Emily. She makes jewelry, you know."

Valerie smiled at Emily. "I had no idea. What kind of jewelry do you make?" She took a sip of her water.

"I make beaded and fused glass necklaces, bracelets, and earrings." Emily sat up straighter and took in every movement of Valerie's expression. "Mostly similar to Mary Dancer's designs. Are you familiar with her work?"

It didn't matter what she said aloud; her expression said loud and clear that she knew all about Mary Dancer's designs. Valerie paused, licking her lips. "Yes, I believe I know her work." She lifted her glass and took another sip of water. Slowly.

Emily waited. This was the perfect opportunity for Valerie to mention the necklace that the man bought for her at the festival. *If* she had nothing to hide. But silence filled the air just as Valerie turned to join the others' conversation.

"So, do you like Mary Dancer's designs?"

"Her work is quite unique. I must see yours sometime." Valerie smiled at Emily, but it looked more like a grimace than a real smile, despite her perfectly white, perfectly straight teeth.

"Actually, now that I think about it . . ." Emily tilted her head. Olivia nudged her, but Emily kept going. "I think I saw you this past weekend at Mary Dancer's booth. At the Finnish festival downtown."

Valerie sputtered her water, then coughed. The conversation at the other end of the table came to an abrupt halt.

Uncle Greg patted Valerie's back. "Are you okay?"

Valerie cleared her throat. Her eyes watered. "I guess the water went down wrong." She blinked rapidly, but her focus remained on Emily. "I'm fine."

A heavy pause filled the dining room. Then Matthew plopped his cup back on the table, and it was as if everyone let out a long breath.

Valerie giggled. "Guess I should be more careful in my drinking."

Uncle Greg grinned and pecked her cheek.

She knew she should just let it go, but Emily couldn't. "So, as I was saying, I think I saw you at the festival this past weekend. I believe you purchased a necklace of Mary Dancer's, right? You were with a friend?"

"Emily!" Dad's tone trembled. "Stop it. We don't interrogate our guests." He threw her a glare before turning to Valerie. "Please excuse my daughter's rudeness."

Emily's cheeks burned, as well as the back of her neck and her chest, and she ducked her head to hide the tears forming in her eyes. She wasn't interrogating Valerie, only asking a legitimate question. A question Valerie was avoiding answering—which was suspicious. "But, Dad, I was just asking Valerie if she—"

"I said that's enough, Emily." The tips of Dad's ears turned red, a surefire way to tell he was mad. Really mad. "Matter of fact, you're excused to your room."

The tears burned the backs of her eyes. Emily scooted back her chair and rose. She left her dishes on the table—something she was never to do—and rushed down the hall to her room before the tears fell and everybody saw them. That would just be the epicness of humiliation.

She flopped onto the bed. Staring up at the ceiling, she sniffled. *Why, God? Why is this happening to me? You know I didn't take the necklace. Why can't you show Dad and the rest of them that I had nothing to do with it?*

Emily punched her pillow and flipped to her stomach. It wasn't fair. She didn't do anything wrong, but now she couldn't even try to clear her name without getting in trouble. It was so wrong. So unfair.

How many times had Dad drilled into her head that life wasn't always fair? Well, in this instance, it was *him* being unfair. If the sheriff wasn't going to find out who the real thief was, someone had to. No one else seemed to care but her and Olivia. Everyone else seemed quite content to let her take the blame—even Naomi, who was usually pretty cool and understanding. No one was willing to give her the benefit of the doubt just because she was a kid.

It was totally unfair.

Volunteering to be a helper to the surf team might not have been the best idea Emily had ever had.

Emily stared at the hamper of wet towels, her heart in her toes. It'd take forever for her to finish the laundry. Coach had told her to wash the towels in the hamper, fold the ones in the dryer, then stack them neatly in the big duffel. He'd barely barked the orders before rushing out to have the surf team run laps to build up their stamina.

How was she supposed to learn anything here in the locker room when everybody else was outside at the track?

Emily struggled to get the cold, wet, heavy towels into the industrial-sized washing machine.

"Need some help?" a male voice said.

She turned to see Brandon in the doorway. "I think I can get it."

He stepped to the basket of towels. "They look heavy."

She got out of the way so he could throw the last of the towels into the washer. "Thanks."

She hadn't been around him much, but he sure was cute. Dark hair and eyes and a nice smile.

He paused. "I just wanted you to know that I don't believe you took that necklace."

Her face flamed, and she looked at the floor. The whole school was talking. About her. All because of Rachel's lies. "Thanks."

"I didn't mean to embarrass you. Sorry."

Her stupid blushes. Emily wanted to melt through the floor. His footsteps moved away, and she peeked up as he disappeared through the doorway. She gulped and looked around for the soap and bleach to load into the washer. Naomi would love one this big—she could wash the family's clothes for an entire week in one load. Thinking about Naomi made Emily frown.

After everyone left last night, Dad and Naomi had brought her into the living room alone to talk. They'd lectured her about grilling Valerie. It wasn't like she was doing it just to be nosy. She was trying to prove her innocence. Not that they cared. Dad was so mad he'd almost refused to sign the permission slip, but Naomi had advised it might give her something to do.

Translation: it might keep her out of trouble.

She would prove them all wrong when she found out what really happened to Mrs. Dancer's necklace.

She added the detergent and bleach, just like Coach had instructed her, then set the washing machine to the longest cycle. After loading the rolling hamper with the towels from the dryer, she moved them to the row between the lockers where she could sit down to fold. This would take some time.

The door creaked open.

"We really appreciate everything you've already given us," Coach said to someone. "The team was on the verge of having to forfeit because of our lack of backup equipment."

Emily held her breath, squeezing a towel to her chest. She couldn't see the coach, but the sounds of two sets of footsteps bounced off the locker room walls.

"I'm just happy to be able to help." A woman's voice, but Emily didn't recognize it.

"We're grateful."

"And I appreciate you keeping the donations anonymous. I'm sure you can understand the delicate position I'm in."

"Of course."

Their footsteps stopped near the coach's office. Emily eased to standing, then crept toward the end of the row of lockers. If she could just get a glimpse . . .

"I hope you understand what your generosity means to the Gitchee Gumee Surfers," Coach said.

Emily leaned a little farther. The light was dimmer in the locker room. Coach flipped on the light in his office, but all she could see was the silhouette of a woman.

"I'm happy knowing I can help. Besides, I don't feel right using this money on me. I want to give back."

So she felt guilty and wanted to use the money to help? Sounded like Emily had a new suspect—if she could just see the woman's face.

Emily inched her way around the end of the lockers, then tiptoed to the next row.

"Those suits and bags were more than enough, but this . . . well, these additional four boards will make all the difference to the team." Coach sounded truly grateful.

"Just go out there and win the championship. Know that while I can't publicly show my preference, I'm rooting for the Gitchee Gumees!" The woman chuckled, but not girly giggly. More husky. "It'd be nice for someone from the mainland to win instead of the Hawaiian teams for once."

Was it Malia? Emily rounded the last row between her and the office. If she could just get a peek . . .

"I agree, but the team mainly wants to ensure they'll beat their archrivals, the Keweenaw Bombers from Houghton. They've beaten up on us for the past five competitions. The team is pumped to beat them this year."

"I hope they do." The woman turned, her back solid to

Emily. "It's a good boost to win. Especially after working so hard for it."

Emily was almost sure it was Malia. She back-stepped to the bench, still holding the towel to her chest. If the woman would only turn around so she could tell for sure.

"Are you sure you don't want me to write you a receipt for all these items? You could at least take them off your taxes," Coach said. His chair scraped against the cracked tile floor behind his desk as he stood.

"No. I didn't want to be a part of this to begin with, but now I have no choice. I'd rather just do what I can for the future surfing stars. It makes me feel better for selling out." No mistaking the down tone of the woman's voice.

Selling out? What did that mean? The whole thing sounded fishy to Emily. Like someone had gotten into something they didn't want people to know about. Something they wanted to keep secret. Maybe even something illegal.

Like stealing a necklace and getting money for it.

"Well, we appreciate it." Coach's office light clicked off. "We aren't too proud to take whatever we can get."

"I'm happy something good can come out of all this."

Footsteps shuffled against the floor.

Emily pressed herself against the cold metal lockers. She sucked in air and held her breath as the woman and Coach passed right in front of her.

They pushed open the door leading to the outside track. Afternoon sun spilled in from the outside, bathing them both in light.

As she'd thought, the anonymous donor was none other than Malia Spencer.

# TEN

"I can't wait to tell Olivia." Emily talked aloud to herself as she finished folding the towels, giving Malia Spencer and Coach plenty of time to clear the area before she exited. After stacking the towels as instructed, she rushed from the locker room and rammed right into Rachel Zinn.

Slammed against the concrete wall, Rachel shoved Emily off her. Hard. "Ugh. Watch where you're going, klutz."

"Sorry, I didn't see you."

"You weren't even looking." Rachel shook her head and twisted her face into a frown. "You are so annoying, Emily!"

Emily blocked her path. "Rachel, I want to know again what you thought I said to Olivia."

"You know perfectly well what you said."

"I sure do, and it wasn't what you told the sheriff. So either you flat-out lied or you twisted something I said."

Rachel put her hands on her hips. "I heard you tell her that you were making a copy of Mary Dancer's necklace so you could switch it and make a lot of money. I don't *think* I heard you say that. I *know* I did."

"But I didn't." Emily popped her hands onto her hips and tried to remember anything she'd said that could have been twisted that way.

"This trying to make everyone think I'm lying is getting old. No one believes you. Gretchen heard you too. Ask her. She'll tell you the same thing." Rachel tossed her blond hair over her shoulder. "Another thing . . . you aren't fooling anyone with this volunteering thing. Everybody knows you're doing it just to get close to Josh." Rachel smoothed her shiny blond hair. "Everybody's laughing at you. Even Josh." She snatched her backpack from the floor. *"Especially* Josh." She turned and marched down the corridor in the direction of the parking lot.

Emily's face burned hotter than a fire poker left in embers overnight. Was it true? Was everybody laughing behind her back? Did they all think she was a thief? Did they think she was just volunteering to get close to a boy? Did *Josh*? All of a sudden, she felt really sick to her stomach. She leaned against the cold concrete wall and closed her eyes. Was she a joke to everyone?

Emily took a breath and followed Rachel. She would *make* her tell the truth. Wasn't there some kind of law against false testimony or something?

The late afternoon September sun blasted against her as soon as she opened the door. Emily blinked rapidly and shielded her eyes with her hand and let them adjust from the dimness of the locker room hallway. She looked around for Rachel but didn't see her. It was as if she'd disappeared.

What was Rachel doing near the locker room, anyway? She should have been in cheerleading practice. The coach and Malia Spencer had left ten to fifteen minutes before, so there wasn't a logical reason for Rachel to be in the hallway.

Unless she was up to no good.

Maybe Emily should focus on figuring out what Rachel would have done with the necklace if she took it. The more she thought about it, the more Emily realized Rachel had the best motive to take the necklace and put Emily's copy in its place, then lie to the sheriff: to get Emily in trouble. She'd been there at both booths during the window of time the necklace went missing. Rachel loved watching Emily get in trouble. But what would she have done with the necklace after switching it? She wouldn't have chanced anyone finding it. Had she hidden it? Gotten rid of it?

The only thing that didn't make sense was Gretchen. Unless Rachel somehow convinced her to back her up. Or made her.

Determined to figure things out, Emily hurried toward her house. She needed to talk to Olivia. Maybe the two of them could find a way to get to Gretchen—to get to the truth.

As she walked home, the gong of the fog bell out in Lake Superior washed over the town. The wind had picked up, and the crash of the waves was oddly soothing.

She'd barely made it inside when Olivia rushed her into the bedroom and shut the door behind them. "How was it? What did you have to do? Did you find out anything? Did you see Josh?"

Emily laughed. "Hang on. Give me a second." She set down her backpack and pulled her hair into a ponytail. "It was boring. I washed, dried, and folded laundry."

"Laundry? You did laundry?"

"The towels from the team's practice in last period, I guess." She shrugged as she sat cross-legged on her bed. "But I did over-hear something interesting. From Malia Spencer."

Olivia's eyes grew wide. "What?"

Emily relayed the conversation she'd overheard, careful not

to leave out any details. When she was done, Olivia plopped on the bed across from her. "What do you think she meant by *selling out,* and what didn't she want to be a part of?"

"I don't know. Whatever it is, it's making money. Enough that she's giving away plenty of it to the surf team. Wet suits, board bags, leashes, and now backup surfboards."

Olivia wrinkled her nose. "You know, my cousin is a surfer out in California, and I hear my aunt tell my mom all the time that the stuff for surfing is expensive. I saw the catalog Aunt Nia left here one time because I actually thought about taking up surfing."

"You're kidding. Let's see how much." Emily rushed down the hall to the computer in the living room where she ran a search for surfing gear. "Wow, look at this, Olivia. Those wet suits average about seventy dollars each. One for each team member totals seven hundred. The surfboard bags run at least fifty each, so for the entire team, that's another five hundred. Add in leashes for the whole team and that's another two hundred."

Olivia tapped the end of her nose with her pointer finger. "That brings the total donation up to about fourteen hundred dollars already. You said they mentioned four surfboards? Even the cheaper competition-grade ones are two hundred each, so that would be another eight hundred bucks, for a grand total of twenty-two hundred dollars. That's over double what Mrs. Dancer's necklace is worth."

Emily hadn't considered all that. It was a lot of money. She and Olivia went back to her bedroom, and she turned her CD player on.

"So you don't think Malia had anything to do with Mrs. Dancer's necklace."

Olivia shook her head. "Not unless something else is missing, and I haven't heard anything like that. The numbers just don't add up." She let out a sigh and leaned back against the mountain of pillows Emily collected at the headboard. "Malia might be into something she doesn't want anyone to know about and she's not happy about being a part of, but it's making too much money for it to be Mrs. Dancer's necklace."

Suspect number two scratched off the list.

Emily couldn't help the disappointment building in her chest. She'd thought they would have hard evidence against someone by now. Something they could take to the sheriff. As it was, Olivia's parents would be home from their cruise on Saturday—just two days away, and then Olivia would go home.

"Hey, I really think we need to check out Valerie more." Olivia sat up and wagged her finger. "Not like you did at the table. Boy, was your dad upset with you."

Emily's face burned at the memory. "Yeah, he almost grounded me for *being rude*. I was being a little nosy, but I was trying not to be too obvious about it. You didn't think I was rude, did you?" It hurt so much that Dad thought she could not only steal something, but be a liar too. She needed to prove to him that she wasn't either.

"I didn't think you were rude. You were just making friendly conversation. Valerie never answered the question about that Mary Dancer necklace that guy bought her either."

"Now I've let her know we know about the guy."

"There wasn't much about her on the Internet. Aside from her modeling stuff."

Emily crossed her arms over her chest. "You looked her up online?"

"I had to find something to keep me busy while you were

doing Josh's laundry." Olivia grinned while heat rushed to Emily's cheeks. "I got busted by Naomi too."

"What?" Emily bolted upright. "What did she say? What did you do?"

"It's okay. She caught me searching for Valerie and asked me about it." Olivia shrugged. "I told her the truth—that I want to be a model someday and Valerie was the first one I'd met in person. I wanted to know more about her." She grinned.

"And Naomi bought that?"

"It's all true." Olivia nodded.

"Wow." Probably a good thing she hadn't been here. Naomi would've seen through Emily in a heartbeat.

"But I didn't find out anything except her modeling stuff."

"Not even some juicy gossip about her?"

"Nothing important. Other than the report that she was recently named the model for Surf's Up."

"Still no clue who the man with her at the festival is?"

Olivia shook her head. "I didn't want to try to find more personal stuff with Naomi in the room."

Emily smiled. "But Naomi isn't here now."

They rushed back to the computer. Images upon images loaded on the pages of articles Emily clicked on. Valerie smiling into the camera. Valerie pouting. Valerie in a bathing suit. Valerie in a wet suit. Valerie with a surfboard. Valerie with a male model.

Olivia shook her head. "See? I told you. Nothing but her modeling stuff."

"Maybe we need to look at older stuff." Emily selected the fifth page on the search engine's main listing.

Another page, much like the ones before, loaded. Emily scrolled down. "Hey, these pictures look older, don't you think?"

Olivia peered over her shoulder. "Yeah, her hair is shorter." She leaned closer to the monitor. "And her nose is wider."

"Are you saying she's had a nose job?"

"Yeah, I think so. Go back even further."

Emily did, then scrolled down that page.

"Stop!"

"You see signs of more plastic surgery?"

"Nope, I see him."

"Who? Uncle Greg?"

"No." Olivia took the mouse from Emily and highlighted a shot of what looked like a party. Valerie stood in the forefront, posing with another girl. "There." She tapped the screen on a man in the background, holding something that looked like a handbag. "Him."

Emily squinted, then sucked in air. "It's the man Valerie was with at the festival."

"Can you print that picture?"

"Sure, but for what?" She set the picture to print.

"I can talk with one of the guys in my computer class. He's always telling me about some program he has that can do searches with a picture. Maybe he can find out who the guy is." Olivia shrugged as the printer hummed. "And as a last resort, at least you'd have the man's photo to give to Sheriff Kaleva."

"Yeah, I'm sure he'll be thrilled with our assistance," Emily said sarcastically before she grabbed the paper off the printer and stared at the image.

"You never know. Or we could give it to Inetta and see if she recognizes him."

"I'd rather not get her involved unless we have to. He seemed nice enough at the festival. I don't want to go around accusing innocent people. I know how that feels."

"I agree."

Emily handed the paper to Olivia. "It's not that clear."

"It's okay. You'd be surprised what this guy can do. He's amazing. Even the teacher asks him for help when her computer messes up."

"Speaking of teachers, I'd better get on my pre-algebra homework. I have two pages." Emily shut down the computer.

Olivia followed her down the hall. "At least you don't have Rachel Zinn in your class to annoy you. That girl goes out of her way to be Mr. Neese's pet when she doesn't even understand basic equations."

She'd almost forgotten. "Speaking of Rachel, I nearly ran her over this afternoon."

"What? Why haven't you told me?" Olivia wore the sternest expression ever. It reminded Emily of Dad when he was really mad.

Emily giggled, then proceeded to tell Olivia about the incident. She finished with, "So now that I think about it, Rachel is my prime suspect. We know for a fact she was at both mine and Mrs. Dancer's booths, she'd take it and then put my copy in its place just to get me in trouble, and for some reason she doesn't like me. It all fits."

"We need to talk to Gretchen and hear her side." Olivia sat backward on the chair in front of Emily's desk. She tapped her painted nails against the wood back. "I can't believe you didn't tell me as soon as you got here. Instead, you bored me with laundry details."

"I'm sorry. My mind's scattered."

"But I think you're right. Something's off with Rachel being there this afternoon." Olivia's nails glimmered under the overhead light. "You really have no idea why she seems to dislike you so much?"

"I don't know. I've tried to figure it out but can't. It's not like I missed one of her birthday parties or something as kids."

"I know. I can't think of anything either. And about the time she started disliking you, she started treating me oddly as well. I mean, she's not as mean to me, but she's not my friend anymore, you know?"

It hurt to remember how Rachel used to be. Emily shrugged. "Yeah, but only toward me and you. Me, mostly. You probably just because you're my best friend."

"Maybe. Have you thought maybe she acts like she does around you because you both have a crush on Josh?"

Heat burned Emily's cheeks, but she shook her head. "She started acting like that long before we even met Josh."

"Hmm." Olivia tilted her head. "Well, you should probably figure that one out. It must be a big deal if she'd do something as serious as stealing a necklace to get you in trouble."

A car door slammed outside just as Charley began barking, his toenails clicking against the kitchen floor.

"Naomi's back." Emily closed her math book and stood. "I do need to figure out why she hates me, but not by asking her."

"You know, Em, if she's willing to steal to get you into trouble, there's no telling what she'll do to you next."

 **ELEVEN**

"You are not going to believe this." Olivia grabbed Emily's arm at the lockers after school on Friday. "Come on." She dragged Emily out into the school's courtyard, then around the corner to the vacant playground. She dropped her backpack on the ground, sat in one of the swings, and waited for Emily to do the same and sit in the swing beside her.

"What? I have to get to the gym." Emily looped her arms around the chains of the swing and noticed Josh and several other members of the surf team heading in that direction. She sat straighter and tucked her hair behind her ears.

Olivia followed Emily's line of focus. "Oh? Well, if doing laundry for Josh is more important than learning who the guy with Valerie was . . ."

Heat flashed up Emily's neck, but she ignored Olivia's sarcasm and stared at her best friend. "You found out?"

Olivia rolled her eyes and stretched her legs, letting the swing gently sway to the right and left. "If you have to go . . ."

"Shut up." Emily giggled and shoved Olivia, knocking her

feet out from under her so she went into a swing. "Come on, Liv, tell me."

Olivia grinned and stopped the swing beside Emily. "Okay. The guy from my computer class, Charles, scanned the picture and tweaked it to make it clearer. Then he loaded it into some program he has that basically searches all graphic images on the Internet and spits back a list of web pages that the image and similar ones are on."

Interesting. "They have programs like that?"

"Apparently." Olivia leaned her swing closer to Emily's as a group of kids walked by.

Once they'd passed, Emily said, "I've seen that on TV, but I didn't realize they were real. I mean, real and where anybody could use them."

"I don't know. What I do know is Charles got several hits on Valerie's friend. Excuse me, her business manager."

"He's her business manager?"

Olivia nodded. "After Charles found his name, which is Kenneth Lancaster, by the way, he did an Internet search to find out information about Mr. Lancaster."

"And? Don't keep me in suspense."

"Are you *sure* you wouldn't rather be doing laundry or something?"

Emily bumped her swing against Olivia's. "Come on. Tell me."

"Well, it seems Mr. Lancaster doesn't have the best reputation in the world."

"Really?"

Olivia nodded. "We found a lot of tabloid reports where models fired him for mishandling their money."

She sucked in her breath. "He stole?" Her pulse sped up at

the thought that maybe this whole nightmare would be over soon.

"The articles didn't exactly say that. Just guessed that he'd mishandled their money."

"What does that mean?"

"I don't know. But there were three different models who fired him using that exact phrase. Oh, and one who not only fired him but has stated she intends to sue him as well."

"For what?"

Olivia shrugged. "We couldn't find out exactly, but Charles said he'd continue to do research for me." She blushed.

Emily grinned. "Does someone have a crush on Charles?" It was fun to pay back a little.

The red in Olivia's face deepened. "No. I mean, he's nice enough, but no. No."

Emily giggled lightheartedly. She so understood her friend's fluster. She felt the same way whenever she talked about Josh. It was worse when she got around him. "I'm just teasing."

"I know." Olivia smiled. "But all the info we found on Mr. Lancaster doesn't explain what he's doing here in Rock Harbor."

"I don't guess agents go on important photo shoots with their clients, huh?"

"No. Think how many clients most modeling agencies have— it'd be impossible for an agent to go on all the important jobs with all their clients."

Made sense. "So why is he here with Valerie for her big Surf's Up shoot?"

"Exactly."

Hmm. It seemed like every time they'd turned over a new lead, they were only hit with more questions. Too many questions, too few answers. And she was running out of time. Olivia's parents would be home tomorrow.

Olivia glanced at the gym. "You'd better get going. Laundry's probably calling." She grinned. "Charles said he'd call if he found out anything. He said he could search better at home anyway because the school has certain websites and search engines blocked."

"I'll see if I can find out anything more about Malia Spencer. See you in a bit." Emily jumped out of the swing, grabbed her backpack, and jogged toward the gym. She quickly went inside, turning down the dark hall to reach the team room just outside the locker room where the coach's office sat.

Seven guys and three girls made up the Gitchee Gumee Surfers. They were already dressed in their old wet suits. They all stopped talking and stared at her as she walked into the team room. Her face burned, and it was as if her feet took root right in the tile floor.

Coach Larson stood and walked beside Emily. "Everyone, this is, uh—" He turned and whispered to her, "What's your name again?"

"Emily O'Reilly," Brandon said.

Emily shot him a quick glance, then looked away. Caycie, a senior who was really good, whispered something to her boyfriend and fellow surfer, Trevor. They both laughed.

Coach glared at the two of them. "Emily has graciously volunteered to help out the team with equipment, water bottles, and stuff."

A couple of the sophomores nodded in her direction. Junior teammate Drake grinned and mock-punched Josh, whose face turned red as fast as Emily's. She dropped her gaze to the floor.

Colleen Coble

Coach tapped his clipboard. "We were just about to head to the surf. You ready to go?"

That shocked the speech back into her. "Me? Why would I go?"

He laughed. "Team, get in the van. Don't forget your leashes this time." He rested a hand on her shoulder. "We *are* a surf team, Emily. Of course most of our practices are on the lake. Come on, grab those towels you put away yesterday and shove them in the bag hanging on my office door. Bring them along." He checked his clipboard. "We're the big white passenger van in the parking lot. Hurry. We only have an hour before practice is over." He turned and exited the door to the hallway.

She headed into the locker room with her pulse throbbing in her throat. It was stupid to get so riled up. Just because she was going to be on the beach didn't mean she had to get even close to the waters of Lake Superior. She'd probably just hand out towels as the team members finished. Emily shoved towels into the bag the coach had mentioned, talking herself into feeling better. Yeah, she wouldn't have to get near the water. She would probably stay near the van, if not inside it.

Emily dragged the heavy bag out of the locker room, down the darkened hallway, and into the parking lot. She tried to lift the bag, carrying it over her shoulder, but with almost twenty towels in a heavy canvas bag, she found she could barely drag the thing.

Brandon ran to meet her. He easily lifted the bag, tossing it over his shoulder like it weighed nothing. "Hey, thanks for volunteering to help out the team. We really appreciate it."

She nodded despite the heat burning her face and neck. "No problem." She fell into step beside him as he made long strides toward the van.

He smiled down at her, flashing a row of perfectly white and

115

perfectly straight teeth in sharp contrast to his darker complexion. The smile reached his almost black eyes. His longish, black hair screamed of his Ojibwa heritage. "I didn't tell you my name earlier. You know, in the laundry room. It's Brandon."

"I know." She could have bit off her tongue as soon as the words were out of her mouth. "I mean, you're the captain, right? The first one ever in middle school." If only the ground would open up and swallow her whole right about now. This was the closest she'd ever been to him, and he was really cute. Maybe even cuter than Josh.

"I am." He swung the bag into the back of the van, then shut the door with a loud bang.

"Come on, team. Time's wasting." Coach shoved himself behind the steering wheel. "Emily, why don't you come sit in the front seat?"

Where was Olivia when she needed her? She climbed into the front seat.

"I have a surprise for you today," Coach said as he pulled into the parking area for the beach.

"Yeah, what's that?" Brandon asked.

Coach parked the van and killed the engine. "You're going to get some pointers from a true pro." He opened his door and stepped down.

Emily opened her door and hopped out as the sliding door opened. The surf team spilled out and grabbed their boards, all talking at once.

"Who's the pro?"

"Would I suffice?" a female voice said behind them.

Everyone, including Emily, turned at the sound of her voice.

Malia Spencer stood in her designer wet suit, holding her championship board and smiling at Coach. "Let's see what this team of yours can do."

"Ms. Spencer!" one of the girls squealed.

The other team members wore excited expressions, and they surrounded her in a loud circle.

Coach nodded. "Do your warm-ups, then hit the water, team."

Ten students raced toward the lake with boards under their arms, sand kicking up behind them. Emily stood awkwardly to the side. "Um, Coach, would you like me to wait at the van?"

"Not at all. Grab the bag of towels and come on down." He turned and walked with Malia behind the surfers.

Grab the bag. Great. Brandon wasn't here to help her get it out of the back of the van. With a sigh, Emily opened the back door and reached for the heavy duffel. It fell on top of her, nearly knocking her off balance. As it was, her arm jammed against the unforgiving metal door.

"Ouch." That was going to leave a bruise for sure. She grabbed the pull strap of the duffel and dredged it across the gritty sand. Maybe she should have thought this volunteering thing through just a little more. She'd rather be doing the laundry than hanging out this close to the lake, dragging a heavy bag.

If she and Olivia could just figure out who took Mary Dancer's necklace and get it back, she could stop this charade of volunteering.

Emily hugged herself, wishing she'd grabbed the jacket from her locker. She got the shivers just thinking about getting in the water, and the air held a hint of moisture that promised rain.

The surf team did their stretches and lined up in a row across the beach. Coach Larson and Malia stood off to the side, whispering. Emily left the heavy bag of towels by the stack of board bags, then crept behind Coach and Malia.

"Is it getting any better?" Coach asked Malia.

"No, but I don't have any choice. I signed the contract."

What contract? Emily inched closer and started braiding her hair, pretending not to even notice them a few feet in front of her.

"Being a spokesperson isn't all bad, Malia. They're paying you well. Very well. And I have to say, we're benefiting from that."

Spokesperson. Ah, that would explain her donations.

"I just feel like I sold out the sport. Once I won the championship, everything changed." Malia's head bent. "It's not about surfing anymore, it's all about selling a product or endorsing something. I hate it."

"It'll be okay. You only have what—until April for the next championship? Then your contract will expire, and you can stop all of it."

Malia's head popped up. "Are you implying I won't win the women's world championship next year?"

Coach chuckled. "Nope. I'm just saying you'll know better than to sign any spokesperson or endorsement contracts again."

Malia laughed and faced Coach. Emily ducked her head as she reached the end of her braid and secured it with the hair tie from around her wrist. She turned away from the two, wanting to ensure if Malia saw her, she wouldn't think Emily had been eavesdropping.

She slowly walked back toward the pile of bags, her mind racing. Malia had nothing to do with Mrs. Dancer's missing necklace. Olivia had been right—the large amount of money Malia had been using to donate items to the school's swim team had nothing to do with the necklace and everything to do with contracts and junk.

Emily plopped down on the sand and sat cross-legged, looking out over the surf. Maybe she'd get lucky and Olivia's friend would find out something about Kenneth Lancaster.

She caught movement out of the corner of her eye. She jerked her head and spied Gretchen walking her dog along the edge of the beach.

Jumping to her feet, Emily brushed the sand from her jeans as she raced toward her. "Gretchen! Gretchen!"

Holding the leash tight, Gretchen faced her. "Hi, Emily." Her voice sounded a bit . . . odd.

"Hey." Emily stopped, bending to pet the tail-wagging chocolate Labrador. "What's his name?"

"Hershey."

Emily straightened and stared at Gretchen. "Listen, I wanted to ask you about what you told the sheriff. About me and Mrs. Dancer's necklace."

Gretchen frowned. "I didn't want to get you in trouble, but I had to tell him what I overheard you say to Olivia when Rachel told him I was there and heard you."

"I never said I planned to steal her necklace." Looking Gretchen in the eye, Emily didn't believe she was lying to get her into trouble.

"But I heard you."

There had to be some logical explanation. "Let me think for a minute."

Hershey tugged on his leash. Gretchen clicked the button to allow the dog more slack. He pressed his nose in the sand and pawed, his tail wagging in the air.

Emily had to figure this out. She wanted her own puppy!

"Okay, when and where do you think you heard me say this?" All the good movie detectives always started at the beginning to solve a case.

"About four weeks ago or so, in the girls' bathroom. The one by the cafeteria. Right after lunch, before the bell rang."

Emily thought hard. That would've been right after she'd seen the news article on the necklace in the paper. "Who all was in the bathroom?"

Gretchen wrinkled her nose as Hershey pawed another area of sand. "Well, me and Rachel were in our stalls because we'd had to wait in line." She pressed a finger to her chin and squinted her eyes. "Sally had just finished washing her hands, I think, because I heard the sink turn off and paper towels pull out of the holder."

None of this sounded familiar to Emily, but it could've been any day of the school week. She and Olivia always went to the bathroom after lunch so Emily could floss. She couldn't stand not to floss after eating.

"I remember I heard the door open and then your voice. You were saying you couldn't wait for the festival. Then I heard Olivia say she was almost finished with her costume."

Still didn't ring any bells with Emily, but sounded like a conversation she and Olivia could've had.

"Then I heard you tell Olivia you were working hard on the copy of Mrs. Dancer's necklace and that you hoped to be finished by the festival so you could swap it and make a lot of money." Gretchen swallowed hard as she tugged Hershey from the water. "I'm sorry, Emily, really I am, but that's what I heard."

There was no way she heard that because Emily hadn't said it.

But she did have the normal routine after lunch. Go to her locker, get her floss, go to the bathroom, floss, rinse . . .

"Did you hear the sink turn on when I was talking to Olivia?"

Gretchen blinked several times. "Yes. Yes, I did."

"When?"

"Um, right after you said you were working hard on the copy."

Hershey barked at the surf team paddling to the beach. "Shh, boy." Gretchen gently tugged on his leash. He stuck his nose back into the sand, sniffing away.

Emily's heartbeat jumped into double time. "Was it on when you think I said I planned to swap the necklace?"

Again, Gretchen blinked rapidly. "Yes. It stayed on until I came out of the stall. You turned it off and wiped your hands and face with a paper towel. I told you hi at the other sink."

*Now* it all made sense. "The water was *on* when you thought you heard me say I could swap the necklace and make a lot of money?"

Gretchen nodded.

"And you were in which stall?"

"The one against the wall."

"The one where all the sounds are kinda muffled because of the concrete wall?"

"I heard you, Emily." Gretchen frowned.

"Is it possible that you *thought* you heard me say 'swap it' when I really said 'sell it'? Think . . . the water was on, you were in the back stall . . . Is it possible?" Emily held her breath.

Gretchen's eyes went wide. "I guess it would've been easy enough to think *sell* was *swap*. I guess."

Emily let out her breath in a *whoosh*. "What happened next? That you remember?"

"You and Olivia told me bye and left, then Rachel came out

of the first stall. She said she never could understand why you, or Mrs. Dancer for that matter, thought anyone would want home-made jewelry."

This was great! It had all been a misunderstanding.

"I'm sorry, Emily. I never meant to get you in trouble. I really thought you'd said *swap* when Rachel told the sheriff that's what you'd said."

Rachel. She'd probably heard Emily right but changed the word to tell the sheriff and convince Gretchen that's what she'd heard—all to get Emily in trouble.

"I know you didn't mean to. Sounds like an honest mistake to me." At least now she had an explanation for the sheriff.

And for Dad.

# TWELVE

Sheriff Kaleva looked stern as he sat across from Emily at the kitchen table. "I understand what you're saying, but Gretchen saying she might've misheard a word isn't exactly evidence of your innocence."

Frustration tightened in Emily's stomach. "But that proves I didn't plan to steal anything, so you can stop trying to figure out what I did with the necklace and try to figure out who really stole it."

Naomi laid a hand over Emily's. "Honey, Mason's been looking for the thief."

"Yeah, but I was his main suspect, and now that there's proof I didn't plan to take the necklace, maybe he can believe that I'm telling the truth about everything and start investigating for real."

"Emily!" Naomi frowned, the corners of her eyes going squinty before she looked at the sheriff. "I'm sorry, Mason."

"No apologies needed." The sheriff met Emily's stare. "I understand your frustration. Trust me, I'm doing my job. We haven't just written off everyone else just because you had motive, means, and opportunity. Despite what you see on television, we don't stop until the truth comes out."

Well, that made her feel better. She nodded. "Thank you, Sheriff Kaleva. I'm sorry if it sounded like I didn't think you were doing your job. I know you're a good sheriff. I just want to clear my name." Emily looked at Naomi. "May I go do my homework now?"

"Sure." Naomi smiled. "And I know you want to tell Olivia."

Emily felt the blush darken her cheeks as she rushed down the hall to her bedroom. She busted inside and told Olivia what the sheriff had said.

"I'm glad." Olivia sat at Emily's desk. "And since you eliminated Malia as a suspect, you can quit your volunteer work with the surf team. You have to study for the Smackdown."

"Yeah." But then she wouldn't get to see Josh every day. Or Brandon. The surf captain had been so nice to her.

"You don't sound as relieved as I thought you would." Olivia chewed on her pencil's eraser. "What gives?"

Emily shrugged and leaned back against her *Phantom of the Opera* pillow. "I really don't know." She pulled the hair tie from the end of her braid and ran her fingers through her hair, unbraiding all the curls. "I won't miss the laundry or being that close to Lake Superior, but it feels wrong to quit something after just two days."

"Did you get to talk with Josh today or something?"

She found it interesting that her face wasn't burning. What did that mean? "No, but Brandon helped me carry the towel bag. And he helped me with the laundry a little."

"Brandon?" Olivia narrowed her eyes. "I thought you liked Josh." Before Emily could reply, Olivia's cell phone rang. She dug in her pocket for the phone. "Maybe it's Charles." She checked the caller ID. "It is." She plopped onto the bed and answered the call. "Hello?"

Emily leaned her head against Olivia's, the phone between them, and listened to the conversation.

"Hi, Olivia. It's me. Charles. Uh, I found out more stuff about Kenneth and Valerie."

"Oh, thank you. What'd you find out?"

"According to stuff I uncovered, Valerie is his last major modeling client. Over the past year, he's lost some of the biggest names in the business. Toya. Maive. Even Cheynne was once one of his clients."

"Not anymore?"

"No. Each one left without publicly stating why. The media only found out when new agents brokered contracts for them."

"Is that unusual?"

"Not so much, but considering how some of the less popular models publicly spoke about him mishandling their money . . . I just thought you might be interested."

"I am. Thank you, Charles. Did you find anything else? Anything that would link him to Rock Harbor?"

"Aside from his attention to his last remaining client and her upcoming photo shoot, nothing."

Olivia moved back to the desk. Emily crossed her arms over her chest and tossed her best friend a confused look. Why didn't she want Emily to listen anymore?

"Did you find out anything about the other thing I asked you about?"

What other thing? Emily cocked her head. What was going on?

"I see."

Olivia wouldn't look at Emily. "Thanks again, Charles."

Olivia smiled. "I'll see you Monday. Bye." She turned off the phone and shoved it back into her pocket.

"What was that about?" She raised her right eyebrow. Olivia hated when Emily did that because she couldn't raise just one. "You and Charles have a secret?"

"Don't be silly." But Olivia blushed. Furiously.

Her best friend *was* keeping a secret! From *her*! She and Olivia hadn't kept things from each other since . . . well, never. Emily's heart thumped hard against her chest. Best friends didn't keep secrets.

"It's nothing." Olivia met her gaze, then lifted her pencil and gnawed at the eraser again.

"If it's nothing, why didn't you want me to listen? What didn't you want me to hear?" It didn't make any sense for Olivia not to tell her everything. They always told each other everything. Well, she always told Olivia. Had her best friend been holding out? For how long? What didn't she know about Olivia Webster?

"Oh, stop looking like an abandoned puppy, will you?" Olivia shook her head. "I just asked Charles to see if he saw anything online linking your uncle to Kenneth Lancaster. He didn't find anything, so there was nothing to tell you."

But she hadn't said . . . "You thought my *uncle* might be involved?"

"Oh, come on, Em. You haven't seen your uncle in how long? Since your dad married Naomi? Then out of the blue he shows up, right after the necklace went missing, and he's with one of the suspects? If he wasn't your uncle, you would've suspected him too."

Well . . . maybe. "I wouldn't have *not* told you I was checking into it, though. You weren't going to tell me at all if Charles hadn't called while I was here."

"No sense in upsetting you when there's nothing to report."

"I wouldn't be upset."

"Right." Olivia waved her hand up and down at Emily. "Like this is you not upset, right?"

"I'm upset right now because you weren't going to tell me." Emily stood and glared at Olivia. "Best friends don't keep secrets, Olivia. Not if they want to stay friends." She stormed from her room into the kitchen.

Keeping secrets like that . . .

Emily opened the fridge and pulled out the iced tea and set it on the counter. Like Naomi's brother could be involved in stealing a necklace? No way. She snatched a plastic cup from the cabinet and filled it halfway with tea.

It was ridiculous. But that she'd kept it a secret bothered Emily even more. What else wasn't Olivia saying?

She opened the fridge door and caught movement from the corner of her eye.

Emily shoved the tea pitcher back on the shelf and stared out the window. What had grabbed her attention? She moved closer to the window, cup of tea in her hand.

The early fall moon cast shadows across the backyard.

There! Was that something right at the edge of the woods behind the house? Had to be big, really big.

Her heart hammered. What was it?

The shadow moved again.

The Windigo! It was real, and it'd come for her. Her grip tightened on the cup. She wanted to scream for Dad and Naomi, but no sound came out when she opened her mouth. It was like something had a hold on her throat.

The motion detector light on the back porch turned on. The cup slipped from Emily's hand and crashed to the floor as the edge of the woods was lit up. Tea sloshed across the floor.

Emily stared at the figure moving.

And then laughed at herself as she realized what it was. A wapiti.

Not a Windigo. Just a big, tall elk.

Emily and Olivia were still not talking the next morning. Last night had been the first time they'd ever gone to bed with any bad feelings between them. They sat across from each other at the breakfast table, silent.

"As soon as you finish, Emily, you need to hop in the shower and get ready. I'll drop you off at practice on my way to work." Dad slurped coffee.

"Practice?"

Dad sighed. He'd been doing that a lot toward her lately. "Practice for History Smackdown starts today. Don't you remember?"

Her school had a two-year winning streak, and they didn't plan to lose now. Every Saturday morning until Christmas vacation, the team would practice for a couple of hours. They'd start back again after the New Year and go every Saturday again until the big contest in March.

She looked at Olivia, who would be going home today, and suddenly wished they hadn't wasted last night being upset with each other, even though she'd gotten a lot of studying done after she'd cleaned up the spilled tea. She nodded at her dad. "Sure. I'll be ready."

"Good. I'm having a big sale at the store and would like to get there as early as I can to make sure Brad has everything under control."

Emily stood and took her dishes to the sink. She washed out her cereal bowl, then stuck it and her spoon in the dishwasher.

Olivia was right behind her and followed her to her room. "You can't still be mad at me, Em. I told you I was sorry. Can't you let it go?"

"I'm sorry, Liv. I guess my feelings were just hurt that you didn't share that you'd asked Charles about Uncle Greg from the get-go."

Olivia gave her a hug. "I should have told you right away, but I really was just trying to save your feelings."

Emily hugged her back. "Let's just agree never to keep secrets from each other. Ever. No matter what."

Olivia pulled back and smiled. "Agreed."

Emily glanced at the clock. "I'd better hurry up and take my shower. Dad will be upset if I'm late." She grabbed a pair of jeans and a long-sleeved henley shirt. "Of course, lately, everything I do makes him upset."

"Is something going on with him? I mean, he can't stay this upset and it just be you. Is there something wrong between him and Naomi?"

She hadn't even considered that, but now that Olivia had mentioned it . . . there had been many times she'd come into a room and both Naomi and Dad had stopped talking immediately. And they'd exchanged strange looks. Oh man. She couldn't take it if they got divorced. She hadn't heard them arguing or anything. Maybe she should ask Timmy. He was even worse about eavesdropping than she was.

"I'm not saying I hope they are, you know. I just remember when my parents were going through their rough patch, it seemed I was always in trouble with one of them for something. Remember?"

"Yeah. You were, like, permanently grounded for almost a month solid."

"So maybe it has nothing to do with you, really." She grinned. "I was thinking some far-fetched stuff. Like maybe I was adopted or something and Dad wanted to tell me and Mom didn't."

"I never did figure out why you thought that." She tipped her head and studied her friend. "Okay, so you don't look like either of them. That's not unusual. I don't look like my mom or dad either. Well, I have my mom's hair, but that's it, thank goodness. I would hate to look like her."

Olivia grinned, but it was a feeble attempt. "You thought you were adopted a time or two."

Emily didn't want to think about Dad and Naomi having problems, but that was all she could think about the entire time it took her to shower, wash her hair, brush and floss her teeth, dress, and pull her hair back into a ponytail. She found Olivia in her bedroom, packing her suitcase. "I hate to bring up bad memories, but back when your folks were having their troubles . . . what were some of the things you remember noticing?"

Olivia sighed and sat down on the bed, a pair of socks forgotten in her hands. "Let's see. Mom cried a lot. Not when she thought I could hear her, of course, but in the bathroom with the shower turned on."

She hadn't heard Naomi crying or anything. Maybe she hadn't been paying attention. She'd start.

"And they'd argue. I could hear their raised voices, but as soon as I came into the room, it'd go quiet as church during silent prayer time."

Emily hadn't heard anyone arguing, but they had gone silent when she came into a room plenty of times.

"And Mom had her sister come stay with us for a long weekend. Mom and Aunt Lydia took long walks that Saturday in the Kitchigami Wilderness Preserve."

It felt like a boulder caught in Emily's throat. Uncle Greg, whom they hadn't seen since the wedding, suddenly appears. What did it all mean?

"Emily! You're going to make me late." Dad's voice rang out from the kitchen. He'd sure been grumpy the past several weeks.

Olivia stood and dropped the socks. "Hey, it's going to be okay. Even if they're having trouble, they'll work it out. Look at how great my parents are now. Their counseling with Pastor Lukkari really brought them closer together than ever before. They're really happy."

"Naomi's going to take you home as soon as your parents get back in town," Emily said. "I promised Bree I'd help her in the lighthouse this afternoon, but I'll call you as soon as I get home."

Olivia waved to her. "I'll talk to you soon."

Emily raced into the kitchen. *God, please, please don't let Dad and Naomi get divorced. Please. I know she's not my real mom, but she is. I love her so much, and she loves me and Timmy.*

Emily rounded the corner just as Dad started to call for her again. "Let's go."

No one was in the kitchen besides her and Dad. "Where's Naomi?"

"Getting Matthew dressed, I suppose. Come on, I'm already later than I'd hoped, and I still have to drop you off at the community center."

Emily and her father rode the short drive to the community center in silence. Mr. Zinn, as the corporate sponsor of the History Smackdown team, had arranged for them to use it. Emily loved walking inside. It was the most beautiful building in all of Rock Harbor with really cool high ceilings and fun corners to explore.

"Have a good time, honey," he said as he pulled up by the center's front door. It was the nicest he'd been to her lately.

Just thinking about the possibility of him and Naomi having problems pushed Emily to lean over and give him a hug. Dad pulled her close to him and planted a kiss on her temple. She gave a final squeeze, then jumped out of the truck. He drove off as she took in a deep breath.

Big chandeliers greeted Emily as she entered. She couldn't quite remember which room Mrs. Kantola, the History Smackdown sponsor, had told her they'd meet in. Was it the first door off the right hallway? That rang a bell for some reason. Emily headed in that direction.

"But, Daddy, I tried. I really did."

Emily froze in the hallway at the sound of Rachel's voice.

Her dad's voice came out in a growl. "Apparently you didn't try hard enough or you would've made the team."

"The others just knew the answers better."

"That's not good enough. You know better. We have to be better than everyone else. No matter what."

"I'm sorry, Daddy." Rachel's sobs made Emily want to cry. "I'll do better next tryout."

"See that you do. I don't want to be disappointed again."

The door on the left opened, and a tearstained Rachel rushed from the room just as Emily pushed open the door across the hall. She ducked inside before Rachel could see her.

"We were wondering if you'd forgotten us, Emily," Mrs. Kantola said. "Please, take a seat."

Emily slipped into a seat, but her mind was on Rachel Zinn. Dad might be a little tough on her, but he'd never come down so hard on her or Timmy.

Poor Rachel.

The attic of the old lighthouse where Bree lived would have been a little spooky except for the illumination from three bare bulbs hanging from the ceiling. Boxes and old furniture were packed into every corner. Emily sneezed and wiped her dusty hands on her jeans.

"Thanks for helping me today," Bree told her. "I hate putting away the summer clothes and getting out the winter ones. At least the kids are entertained." She wore jeans and a Detroit Tigers sweatshirt. A kerchief covered her curls.

Emily spared a glance at her charges just to make sure they weren't getting in any trouble. The twins were playing with their dolls in the corner. They pulled old baby clothes out of a trunk and were happily entertained. "It's a cool place."

"I've spent hours exploring. The original Fresnel lens for the light tower was the best find, but I also found a sea captain uniform from the 1850s. And a ball dress that I wore to a masquerade party once." She smiled. "Look at those two." She gestured to Samson curled in the corner with her puppy sprawled across him.

"I want him to be just like Samson." *If* she got to have him. She *had* to figure out who took the necklace so her puppy could come home with her.

"It's going to take a lot of hard work for both of you. That kind of training doesn't happen overnight. It will take years."

"I know, and I'm ready for it. What can I do to help him get started? If I get him, of course."

"Have Timmy hide and let him go find him. Always use a scent article. He'll get used to playing hide-and-seek and will love it if you make it into a game."

"How old was Samson when you started training him?"

"About six months old. He was a natural at it."

"You think my puppy has a gift like Samson?" Wow. That'd be way awesome.

Bree nodded. "I'm sure of it." She shoved a box under the eaves, then studied Emily's face. "Is everything all right? Are you still upset about the necklace?"

Emily shrugged. "Everyone believes I took it, especially since two girls told the sheriff they heard me say I'd planned to take it." She shook her head. "I didn't."

"I know." Bree gave her a soft smile. "Have you talked with the girls? I'm sure it's all a misunderstanding."

Emily sighed and handed her a box to stash. "Yeah, and one of them admitted she may have misheard, but that's not enough to clear my name. You've investigated lots of mysteries. How can I find the real thief?"

Bree put the box on the one she'd just set down. "Honey, this isn't your job. The sheriff will handle it. Investigations can be dangerous. I wouldn't want to see you get hurt." She studied Emily's face. "Have you been investigating on your own?"

Emily's face got hot. "Just a little. I'm not getting anywhere, though."

"Does your dad know you're poking into things?"

Emily looked over at the twins again. "Well, not really." Guilt pricked her for not telling everyone that she was working with Inetta. She should have told Dad or Naomi.

"What have you found out so far?"

Emily listed the suspects she'd had, who she'd eliminated, and how.

"I'm impressed, Emily," Bree said. "I never would have guessed you would have such a flair for investigation."

That was high praise coming from such a top-notch investigator as Bree. Emily sneaked another glance at the twins, who were still occupied with the doll clothes. "But I'm stuck now. I don't know what to check next."

"First off, I'd talk to Rachel. Ask her why she's angry with you and apologize for any way you've hurt her feelings. You need to clear the air between the two of you, and God says when you know someone is offended that you need to go to them and try to resolve it."

"He does?" Emily didn't like the sound of that. She knew all about not holding a grudge against others, but was it *her* responsibility to go to someone who was mad at her?

"Read Matthew 5:23–25. It tells you if you are giving God a gift and remember that your brother has something against you that you should stop what you're doing and be reconciled. So basically God doesn't even want you giving him anything until you set things right."

Emily sighed. "That doesn't seem fair, and it's going to be super hard."

Bree smiled. "It's good for your character. And God is more concerned about your character than anything."

"Okay, okay, I'll do it."

"Good. And tell her that you think she misunderstood what you said. Maybe Gretchen would agree to talk to her too."

"Maybe."

Bree studied Emily's expression again. "Is the gloomy face you're wearing about the prospect of talking to Rachel, or is something else bothering you?" Bree bent over to adjust the clothing in a box so the lid fit better.

Emily bit her lip. "It's about my dad and Naomi."

Bree straightened. "What about them?"

"This is just between us, okay?" Emily waited until Bree nodded. "I think they're getting a divorce."

Bree gaped. "Oh, honey, whatever gave you that idea?"

"They're acting weird. They've been tense all the time. And they stop talking when I come into the room, but I've heard them raise their voices like they're upset. I remember my mom and dad acting like that before my mom left."

Bree put her hand on Emily's shoulder. "You should talk to them about your fears. I'm positive it's nothing like that. If you tell your dad you're worried, he'll tell you what's going on."

Emily saw something in Bree's face, a knowledge. "Do *you* know what's going on?"

Bree bent over the box again. "This is something you should talk to your dad and Naomi about."

Dread squeezed Emily's chest. Bree must know something. If it wasn't divorce, then maybe one of them *was* sick. Maybe one of them had cancer or something terrible. She couldn't bear the thought.

She swallowed hard. "I-I'll talk to them."

Bree straightened. "Good. Honesty is always best. You can drive yourself crazy thinking things that aren't true when all it would take to set your mind at ease would be to talk things out."

"I guess." Emily wasn't looking forward to any of it. Maybe she shouldn't have brought up the subject at all.

# THIRTEEN

Emily put her history book away and went to see her brother. "I need to talk to you." She stepped into Timmy's room and shut the door behind her. Charley looked up from his nap on the bed.

"I didn't do anything." Timmy gently set the half-painted airplane model onto its stand on the desk.

Emily gave a weak smile and sat at the foot of her brother's bed. Charley inched down and pushed his head into her lap, his big brown eyes silently begging her to pet him. She dug her fingers into the lovable golden retriever's silky fur. "I heard you last night, crying out. Nightmare?"

Timmy looked down. "Yeah."

"Why didn't you tell anyone you were having them again?"

He shrugged with only one shoulder and stared at the floor. "I'm too old for nightmares. I'm not a baby anymore."

"Hey, everybody has scary dreams. It has nothing to do with age."

"Do you?" Timmy lifted his head and met her stare.

She started to tell him about the steady nightmares she'd had about the Windigo after their babysitter had scared her silly, but she couldn't because then she'd have to admit she hadn't outgrown them. "Sometimes I do." She remembered the dream she'd had last night and straightened her back. "They aren't fun."

"What are your nightmares about?"

"I dreamed I fell into the lake and drowned. That was a nightmare for sure." She'd awakened in a cold sweat, her heart hammering.

"Wow. You dreamed you died?" Her little brother's eyes were wide.

She nodded. "Do you ever dream that?"

Timmy nodded. "I dream Mom is there, holding my insulin, and won't give me the shot." He shivered.

Emily curled her hands into fists. How dare their mother cause such fear in a little boy? All because she'd altered his medication and made him sick. *On purpose.* What kind of mother did that?

Theirs.

She put her arm around his shoulders and squeezed. "It's okay, Timmy. Dad and Naomi won't let her hurt you again." She squeezed tighter. "And I won't either."

It was unfair that Timmy had to deal with all this.

*God, it's me again. This time I'm not asking you for anything for me. Just for Timmy. He's scared and shouldn't be. It's not his fault our mother is what she is. You've got to help Timmy. I don't know what to do for him. Please. Help him.*

She hugged him. "Have you talked to Dad or Naomi about the nightmares at all?"

He looked down at the floor. "Dad's been so busy at work lately. He hasn't even come with me to the field to fly my planes."

That was unusual. Dad usually made time to fly the model airplanes with Timmy at least once a week. It was their father-and-son bonding time. Emily had been jealous of it more than once.

Maybe Dad hadn't made the time not because he'd been busy at the store, but because he and Naomi were having problems. But Emily couldn't just ask Timmy if he'd overheard any arguments. He was obviously stressed enough. More stress could affect his diabetes.

"I know what you mean." She drew a deep breath, then let it out slowly. "You know, the other night I must've been dreaming because I could have sworn I heard Naomi crying in the bathroom in the middle of the night." Emily held her breath, waiting to see if Timmy would volunteer any confirmation.

He chewed his bottom lip—a sure sign he was worrying about something.

"Have you heard Naomi doing anything strange like that?"

Timmy opened his mouth like he was going to say something, paused, then slowly shook his head. "I haven't heard her crying."

"But you have seen or heard something strange with her?"

He nodded.

This was worse than benchmark tests. "What?"

"I wasn't really eavesdropping, I just couldn't help hearing her and Dad in the kitchen from the pantry." He hung his head. "I was sneaking some treats for Charley—"

The dog lifted his head at the word *treats*. Emily rubbed between his ears, and he laid his head down again but kept a careful watch on Timmy with his soulful eyes.

"And I heard Naomi tell Dad that she wouldn't go through it again. She used her serious voice."

It? "She wouldn't go through what again?"

"I don't know. I didn't hear anything before that."

That could be just about anything. "What did Dad say?"

"He said he didn't want it to come to it, but if he had to go the legal route, he would."

A legal route? That didn't sound good at all. "What else?"

"Naomi just said they'd consider their options."

"What options?"

Timmy shrugged. "I don't know. You and Olivia came into the kitchen, and Dad went to wash up for dinner."

What did it all mean? She didn't have time to think about it as her cell phone buzzed in her pocket. She had a text. She stood and gave her brother a gentle hug. "Don't worry about it. Everything's gonna be okay."

He nodded, but his expression said he didn't believe her.

She couldn't blame him—she had no way of knowing what would happen.

"And if you wake up with any nightmares, you let me know, okay?"

He nodded.

"Promise me, Timmy." She put her hands on her hips.

"I promise."

She smiled and headed back to her room. She checked her phone and read the message from Olivia: **Charles said nothing new. miss you**

Emily quickly texted back: **ok will talk 2 u @church. miss you**

"Timmy! Emily!" Dad hollered from the living room.

Calling both of them? Must be important. Emily licked her lips as she shoved her phone back into her pocket.

*God, it's me again. I just wanted to ask you not to let my parents break up. Timmy needs Naomi. I need Naomi.*

She and Timmy met in the hall and headed into the living room together.

Naomi walked into the room with big bowls of popcorn. "It's movie night. I have popcorn!"

Dad waved the remote control. "It's Naomi's turn to choose the movie, right?"

Emily smiled and let out a huge sigh of relief. If Dad and Naomi remembered movie night, and even whose turn it was to pick the movie, they couldn't be on the brink of breaking up, right?

Naomi was smiling, a lighthearted tip to her lips that Emily hadn't seen in a while. "I choose *The Princess Bride*."

They all groaned. "Again?" Emily hit her head with a pillow. "We've only watched that thing a thousand times."

"It's my favorite movie." Naomi hugged her. "And it's not like we haven't had to watch *Phantom of the Opera* as many times."

Emily hugged her back, glad to see some joy in her. "Okay, okay. But next week is my turn."

Timmy snuggled between Dad and Naomi, while Emily pulled out the overstuffed pillows to prop against the couch and lean on. As Dad started the movie, Emily grabbed a big handful of the buttery popcorn. Maybe she and Olivia had been mistaken. Probably. All this missing necklace business had Emily all messed up.

The doorbell rang.

Dad paused the movie as Naomi opened the front door.

Sheriff Kaleva stood in the doorway, his hat in his hands. "Sorry to bother you on a Saturday night, but Bree's out of town on another search."

"What is it?" Naomi's back straightened as Charley went to her side.

"It's Rachel Zinn. She's missing. We need you and Charley to help, Naomi."

Naomi pressed her foot to the accelerator of the SUV. Emily pressed her lips together, not daring to do anything to draw attention to herself as they left the lake behind and raced forward along the rutted dirt track. It was a miracle Naomi and Dad had even let her help, but with Bree out of town, Naomi and Charley *were* the Kitchigami K-9 Search and Rescue team.

Emily steadied herself against the door's armrest and looked over her shoulder at Charley safely confined in his kennel. The Kitchigami Wilderness Preserve lay to the east, past Miser, a drive of only fifteen miles or so, but it felt much longer tonight.

Emily shivered under the orange vest Naomi had loaned her. Her throat was tighter than the vest's buckles.

*God, please keep Rachel safe. I know she's mean to me and all, but please . . . I don't want her to get hurt.*

"Here's what we know," Naomi said. "Rachel's dad said she didn't come home in time for dinner. He's called all her friends and checked everywhere: the community center, the library, the café, even the Coffee Place . . . No sign of her, but one of her classmates said his family had given her a ride to the campground. He'd last seen her at the picnic area out here."

Emily swallowed against a dry mouth.

"Mr. Zinn said the last time he saw her was around ten this morning. Calls to her cell phone are going straight to voice mail," Naomi said.

Emily remembered the look on Rachel's face when she ran away from her father's harsh words. Should she tell Naomi?

"One of her friends said she'd asked Rachel to go shopping with her, but Rachel told her she had to study." Naomi continued, "Mr. Zinn says he doesn't think Rachel went anywhere to study."

"And not here for sure," Emily muttered.

Naomi looked at her curiously. "You know something about Rachel? If you do, Emily, now's the time to tell me. Time's of the essence."

Emily looked out the window. She remembered when she and Timmy were lost in the woods and Bree and Naomi had to come find them. It'd been cold and scary. "I saw Rachel leaving the community center this morning."

"Did she tell you where she was going?" Naomi tapped the steering wheel with impatient fingers, as if that would make the SUV go faster over the bumpy, rutted road.

"I didn't talk to her. She didn't even see me. She was upset."

"Upset?"

As Naomi slowed and turned onto the access road that would take them back to the campground parking lot, Emily told her about what she'd overheard and seen.

Naomi pulled into the parking lot, making humming noises. That meant she was working something out in her mind. The SUV's headlamps caught a lot of people moving about. There was an assortment of searchers, ranging from teenagers to adults. A big tent had already been set up with a generator and huge floodlights that kept the whole area lit. When one of their own was threatened, Rock Harbor residents pulled together. But the searchers hadn't had any luck or they wouldn't have had to bring in the search-and-rescue team.

Emily followed Naomi out of the SUV, attached Charley's

leash, and shrugged on the ready-kit backpacks, fully outfitted with a first aid kit, a small plastic tarp, energy bars, a flashlight, flares, bug repellant, towelettes, a compass, a Swiss Army knife, a radio, a topographic map of the area, a canteen, sunglasses, sunscreen, and every other item anyone could need on a search.

"Over here, Naomi." Sheriff Kaleva motioned them over to a group of deputies and park rangers.

Naomi headed toward the group. Emily followed in silence.

Mr. Zinn turned to face their approach. Pain contorted his steely features. "Please, you've got to find her!" His hands trembled as the torment in his eyes spoke of his fear of loss more clearly than his words.

Naomi put a comforting hand on his arm. "We'll find her, Mr. Zinn. Charley is well trained, and he's in familiar territory."

"I hope so. Since her mother died, she's all I have." He shook his head. "She doesn't even answer her cell phone. She's never without that thing."

"I need something of hers. Something she wore recently."

"I have her sweater she wore this morning in the car. Will that work?"

Naomi nodded. "Perfect." She handed him a paper bag and a plastic glove. "Put the sweater in this and don't touch it with your bare hand."

He rushed to get it, returning in a flash to hand her the bag. When they peered into the bag, Emily saw a sweater she was very familiar with. It was Rachel's cheerleading squad sweater.

Naomi gave Mr. Zinn a smile. "Stay close to base. Rachel might be scared when we find her, and you'll need to be in a position to get to her quickly when she's found. Try to stay calm. We'll find her."

Mr. Zinn nodded, but his fearful gaze flickered from Emily to Naomi. "I want to do something."

"Pray," Naomi advised.

Naomi's answer to everything was prayer. Prayer had done little for Emily's own desperate pleas lately to clear her name. In the midst of Rachel going missing—and Emily knew how scary and hard that could be—she realized her pleas had been pretty self-centered.

*God, I'm sorry I've been selfish. Please keep Rachel safe. That's what's most important right now. Even more than proving I'm innocent.*

When she looked around again, she saw Brandon walking toward her, and her heart skipped. She waited until he reached her. "You're helping with the search?"

He nodded. "Want me to come with you?"

"Sure."

"Let's go." Naomi flipped on her flashlight and headed toward the campground with Charley, Emily following, her own flashlight burning. "Remember, you have to keep up with me. I won't be able to stop and keep track of you."

Emily nodded and fell into step beside Brandon.

"If we get separated, I have my cell phone on. Check and make sure yours is fully charged," Naomi told them.

Doing as instructed, Emily nodded at Naomi. "Yep, 98 percent."

"Okay. And keep your flashlight burning at all times. It's going to be hard enough searching in the dark without Samson." She knelt beside Charley and held the bag containing Rachel's sweater under his nose.

Charley whined and strained at the leash. Naomi released his lead and dropped her arm. "Search!" she commanded.

The dog bounded toward the trees. He ran back and forth, his muzzle in the air. Charley wasn't a bloodhound but an air scenter. He worked in a *Z* pattern, scenting the air until he could catch a hint of the one scent he sought.

Charley's tail stiffened, and he turned and raced toward the creek.

"He's caught it!" Naomi said, running after her dog. Her flashlight beam bounced as she ran with Brandon on her heels.

Emily ran to catch up, her heart thumping. *God, please keep Rachel safe until we can find her. Please.*

 **FOURTEEN**

The sounds of people and cars fell away as though they had slipped into another world. The forest closed in around them. The wind whispered through the trees, sounding like a high-pitched scream. The moon was all but blocked by the density of the forest. The muffled sounds of insects and small animals scurrying made Emily shiver as she ran to keep up with Naomi, who trailed Charley.

Brandon's face was white. "Did you hear that?"

She nodded. "My old babysitter used to tell me it was the Windigo out on the prowl."

He looked uneasy. "Maybe it is."

"Are you trying to scare me?"

He grinned but still looked uneasy. "Maybe."

Naomi stopped ahead of them. "Let's take a break. Charley needs a drink." She poured water from her bottle into her cupped palm and let the dog lap it up.

After almost an hour, Emily was glad to sit on an old log with Naomi and Brandon. She was tired of thrashing behind Charley in the vegetation. And the night was so dark, it was creepy. Charley had lost the scent about ten minutes ago. He crisscrossed the clearing, searching for the lost trail with his muzzle in the air.

Naomi handed Emily the water bottle and pushed away a lock of hair that had escaped her braid.

Emily took a long sip, then handed it back to Naomi.

Naomi grinned and put the water bottle back in her bag. "Time to get moving again. Charley's lost the trail." She whistled, and Charley came to her. He shook himself. She knelt and took his golden head in her hands and stared into his dark eyes. "I know you're trying, buddy, and that it's hard without Samson here," she whispered.

He whined and sniffed the air as if determined not to let her down. Or Samson. He ran ahead, then began to bark.

Emily's adrenaline kicked into overdrive as Naomi leaped to her feet. "He's found the scent again."

Fatigue forgotten, Emily followed Naomi and Charley again with Brandon beside her. The dog bounded toward a steep hill covered with vines and the small trunks of new-growth pine and birch. Naomi and Emily followed, trying to keep the dog in sight with their flashlights.

Emily loved to watch Charley and Samson work. Over the summer, she'd spent at least three days every week at the training school. All the "students" practiced in the meadow at the top of the hill and worked by zigzagging in a circle with their noses held high as they tried to catch the scent cone. It was funny at times, when one dog would catch the scent of a rabbit instead and try to give chase. She couldn't wait to get her puppy and start training him to search. She had to clear her name and get that puppy. She just had to.

Suddenly Charley began to bark, then ran toward an object along the riverbank. Emily shone her flashlight where the dog ran. A flash of red drew her attention, and Emily squinted as she settled the beam of light on the object. "What's that, Naomi?"

"I think it's a backpack!" Naomi ran after Charley.

Emily ran faster, trying to keep up. The light from their flashlights bounced and bobbed. The dog picked up a stick, his signal of a find, and brought it to Naomi. She paused long enough to praise her dog, then followed him to the backpack.

Naomi turned to Emily and Brandon. "This is Rachel's. She's been here." She bent to Charley. "Good boy." She held the open backpack under his nose, letting him get a good whiff. "Search!" she commanded as she stood.

Charley took off. Naomi slung the red pack over her shoulder, then she was running after the dog, the light from her flashlight bouncing. Brandon followed them.

Emily climbed another hill, stopping to catch her breath as she spied Charley in her flashlight's beam, zigzagging at the bottom. He'd lost the scent. Or had Rachel doubled back? She and Timmy had done that when they'd been lost in the woods. Not on purpose, but because they'd gotten turned around. They'd been "loster than lost," as Timmy had claimed.

Emily smiled at the memory of Timmy's phrase, then considered maybe Rachel had gotten turned around as well. Perhaps that was why Charley went back and forth as he tried to keep the scent. Before Emily could holler at Naomi, Charley bounded off in another direction and Naomi rushed to follow, Brandon close on their heels.

Emily shrugged out of the ready-kit backpack and hung it loosely over her arm. The wind whistled through the trees. She shined the light on the path she'd taken, looking for any movement. All those stories about the Windigo played across her mind. What if the Windigo was real?

Her heart pounded. No, monsters weren't real. She knew that. Emily let out a slow breath and started down the hill. She stepped on a rock and felt her ankle give. She threw her hand out, hoping to grab a limb, a tree, a vine . . . anything. Her fingers met with nothing but air. And then her arms pinwheeled as she pitched forward. There was nothing to grab hold of, and she screamed.

Her right shoulder slammed against the rocky ground. Pain radiated across her back and up her neck. The momentum of her fall threw her legs over her head, then her head over her legs, over and over as she tumbled down the hill.

Suddenly, she was jerked to a stop as something sharp grabbed at her hair and jacket and scraped across her skin. Emily couldn't even scream as the air was knocked from her lungs. Her hair jerked her head sideways. *It's the Windigo*, she thought frantically, too terrified to even reach up and try to pull herself free. Maybe it was dragging her to its cave. Emily found her voice and shrieked.

With every inch of courage she had, Emily pulled hard. She heard a loud rip of fabric as she tore her jacket, and her hair pulled painfully before it finally gave and she rolled free. She tumbled farther down the hill before her shoulder slammed into a stump and she came to a stop.

She let out a long breath as her heart raced. She sat up, hissing in pain. Her shoulder was on fire, but she knew she couldn't stay where she was. What if the Windigo was coming after her? Something rustled in the trees, and goose bumps pebbled her arms as she stood. "Wh-who's there?" A bunny hopped across the path. She felt almost faint with relief. Not the Windigo.

*Thank you, Lord.*

Emily groaned as the pain in her right shoulder increased. She found her flashlight on the ground nearby and turned it on with her left arm. She shone the light on her painful arm. Her sleeve was torn, and a really nasty, deep scratch bled below it.

Emily jerked her flashlight around—there was no sign of Naomi, Brandon, or the Windigo. She couldn't even hear Charley barking or thrashing through the woods. It was just her, hurt and alone, like last time. Except last time, she'd had Timmy with her. She'd had to be strong for him. Now she had no one.

Except God.

*I'm so glad you're here, God.* She worked her way up to sitting on the stump, testing her legs. So far, so good. She stood and wobbled for a minute, then felt the earth straighten under her feet. She swung her flashlight around up the hill, looking for a way back up. It was too steep for her to climb up with her hurt shoulder. Then she spotted a bush with a piece of her jacket hanging from its bare branches. She giggled nervously. That's what she'd been caught on—at least it hadn't been the Windigo! She was glad no one had been around to see her fighting with a bush—how embarrassing! Almost as embarrassing as it was going to be to call Naomi and Brandon and admit she was lost.

Emily was so relieved that she prayed aloud, "Thanks, God. Now, if you could just help me find Naomi without me having to call and tell her I got lost . . ."

"Who are you talking to, Emily?"

Emily spun around as best she could, considering she was still a little dizzy from her fall, and shone her flashlight at

Rachel Zinn. "Where have you been, Rachel? Your father's worried sick, and the sheriff and the search-and-rescue team are looking for you."

"Get that light out of my eyes." Rachel shielded her eyes with her hand, her own flashlight pointing downward.

"Oh. Sorry." Emily moved the light. "Everybody's looking for you. Are you okay?" Rachel didn't look hurt. Or scared. Emily wasn't feeling too sorry for her at the moment.

"I just wanted some time alone. To think." Rachel stuck out her chin and tossed her hair over her shoulder in that annoying way of hers.

"So you come out in the middle of the woods, in the dark?" Emily glanced around. Maybe Rachel had hidden the necklace out here.

"No." Even in the dim glow from the flashlights, Rachel looked annoyed. "I didn't realize it was so late. By the time I needed to head home, it'd gotten dark and . . ." Her expression turned to one Emily identified all too well with: embarrassment.

"You got turned around? It happens to most everybody, you know," Emily said softly as she lowered herself back down to the stump. Her arm and shoulder hurt something awful. Where had the ready-kit backpack fallen?

"I did. And then . . . well, my cell battery died so I couldn't even call anyone." Rachel's voice cracked.

"Your dad is worried sick." Emily felt around for her cell phone. There it was in her pocket.

"Yeah. Sure. Right." Rachel sat down on the ground and pulled her knees to her chest. "He'd be better off without me being such a disappointment to him."

"Don't say that. He told Naomi that you were all he had left."

Did Mr. Zinn not let Rachel know how much she meant to him? Even when Dad was mad at her, he always let her know he loved her. Despite Rachel's bratty behavior, Emily felt sorry for her. Emily moved to reach for Rachel's hand but stopped. She pulled out her cell and dialed Naomi's number.

"He sure doesn't act like he cares." Rachel rested her cheek on her knees.

The call was picked up on the other end. "Emily! Where are you? Are you okay?" Naomi sounded as worried as Mr. Zinn had.

Emily's throat tightened at the concern in Naomi's voice. Right now, she felt like a little kid, and all she wanted to do was burrow into Naomi's arms. "I'm fine. Kinda. I fell down a hill and cut myself, but I'm okay."

"Oh, thank the Lord that you're okay. I couldn't find you and nearly panicked. I'm trying to round up Charley, but the scent cone must be eluding him because I swear we're going back the way we came. Where are you?"

"I'm at the base of the hill from where we sat on the log and had water."

Naomi's shrill whistle sounded over the connection. "I know the area. We're on the way. Stay where you are."

"Okay. Naomi?"

"Yeah?"

"Rachel's with me."

"Is she hurt?"

She glanced over at Rachel, still curled up. "No." Her feelings were, but she looked to be physically better off than Emily.

"I'm on my way."

Emily shoved her cell back into her pocket and stared down at Rachel. She didn't know how to comfort her. After all, she'd overheard Mr. Zinn and had been really grateful he wasn't her dad. Maybe a change of subject would help. "Rachel, I know this probably isn't the best time, but I'm just wondering . . ."

Rachel lifted her head and shone her flashlight at Emily's feet. "Yeah?"

"Wh-why do you hate me so much?" She licked her dry lips. Olivia would be proud—being direct without sarcasm.

"I don't *hate* you."

"I know you think I planned to steal Mrs. Dancer's necklace, but you're wrong. You and Gretchen misheard me with the water running and the echoes in the bathroom. I said I planned to *sell* my copy of the necklace, not *swap* it. Gretchen's already helped me figure that out."

Rachel tilted her chin up. "I know what I heard."

"I wouldn't steal, Rachel. Really. I think you know me better than that. And we used to be friends."

Rachel looked away. "Maybe. I mean . . . I guess you maybe could've said *sell*."

Emily swallowed, grateful the darkness hid her blush. "You've been really mean to me for a while now. You look at me like I'm a nasty bug you need to squish or something." She shook her head. "We were good friends before middle school. I don't know what I did to make you hate me. Whatever it was, I don't even know I did it."

Rachel laughed. "You just don't get it, do you?"

Why was she laughing? Emily bit her tongue. She'd tried to be sincere.

"Ever since you beat me in the fifth-grade spelling bee, my dad has compared me to you. Every single awards ceremony, you'd get at least one more award than I did. Every time I turned around, I got to hear how smart you were. Why couldn't I apply myself as much as Donovan O'Reilly's little girl?" Rachel's voice turned as cold as normal. "I get sick of hearing how perfect you are, day in and day out."

"Come on. Rachel, you can't be serious. You're president of our class. You're a JV cheerleader. You're Miss Popular." She waved a hand at her, then winced with the burning. "And look at you—you're beautiful. Everyone thinks so." Blond hair, blue eyes, and petite as opposed to uncontrollable dark curls, curves that made Emily blush, and an awkward height that often put her taller than some of the boys her age.

Rachel snorted. "Oh please—I would kill to look like you. You have that gorgeous curly hair, you're tall, and you actually have curves. All of the guys think you're pretty. And none of my activities are good enough for my father." She stretched her legs out in front of her, shoving leaves across the ground, and mimicked her father's grave tone. "Colleges don't care who the cheerleaders or popular kids were, Rachel, but they all take notice of which students got the most scholarships. Who won the most academic awards. Who starred in the History Smackdown win." She stood. "Dad doesn't give me any credit. It's never good enough. Not when he has *you* to compare me to. Just when I think I've done something to make him proud, you have to go out and one-up me. I think he wishes he had you for a daughter instead of me."

Like that was her fault? Emily swallowed the bitter reply sitting on the tip of her tongue. She remembered how she'd felt when her dad had believed Rachel over her—it hurt. It must hurt even worse to feel that your dad would rather have a different daughter—even if it wasn't true.

"I'm sorry. I never intend to one-up anyone. Really." And she was. None of this was her fault, but she could understand how Rachel felt. It wasn't Rachel's fault either. "And I saw your dad before we came to look for you. He was a mess. He loves you, Rachel, and I know he's proud of you. I want my dad to be proud of me too, you know—that's part of why I study really hard. But I do it for me too."

Rachel stared at her for a long moment.

Emily sighed. "Dads are supposed to push us, I guess. Your dad was really worried, Rachel. I know he loves you, just like my dad loves me. I was just trying to work hard for my dad the way you do for yours. I've never tried to make you look bad or show you up on purpose. And I've never understood why we stopped being friends. It really hurt my feelings."

Rachel chewed her lip, then slowly nodded. "I guess you're right. I'm sorry for being so mean. I've just been so angry, but it was wrong to take it out on you." She shone her flashlight on Emily. "Oh my goodness. Your arm." She rushed to Emily's side, shining the light on the scratch.

It hadn't stopped bleeding entirely but had slowed considerably. It sure hurt like everything, though.

"That looks pretty deep. You might even need stitches." Rachel looked around. "Do you have anything to put on this?"

"Yeah." She flashed the light around and spied the ready-kit backpack on the ground about three feet away. She nodded toward it. "That pack. Open up the center part. There should be a first aid kit in there. Do guys really think I'm pretty?"

"Yeah, they do," Rachel said. "I think Brandon really likes you."

Emily blushed.

Charley barked. Close.

Rachel jumped.

"It's just my stepmom and her SAR dog."

Rachel gave a nervous smile. "Thought it might be the Windigo, you know?" She chuckled. "Did you believe that story as a kid?"

Emily nodded. "Every last word. I was terrified." And for a little while tonight, she'd thought maybe the Windigo had come for her at last. She shivered.

"It's crazy, the legends from this county."

Charley bounded up to Emily, jumping up on her and nearly knocking her off the stump. "Whoa, boy."

Naomi rushed to Emily and gave her a hug. "Oh my. We'd better treat this before we head out." She took the first aid kit from Rachel. "I called the sheriff. He's let your father know we found you and that you're all right. He's very relieved." She pulled presoaked Betadine towelettes from packages and squeezed them over Emily's scratch.

Coldness seeped into her, followed immediately by stinging. "Ouch. Where's Brandon?"

"Sorry." Naomi reached for the antibacterial cream and oozed some over the wound, then covered it with a large bandage. "He went to lead the sheriff here. There. That'll have to do until we get out of here." She shoved the supplies back into the first aid kit, then jammed it all back into the pack and slung it on her back. "Are you girls ready?"

Rachel nodded. Emily stood slowly. "Yeah."

"Are you sure you're okay to walk?"

"I'm fine. My shoulder is killing me and my ankle's a little sore, but I can walk on it."

Naomi studied her for a minute, then nodded and started out. "Rachel, why don't you tell me how you ended up out here in the first place?"

Emily smiled as she listened to Rachel explain she'd just come out to be alone and got turned around.

*Thank you, God, for watching out for both of us. And for giving Rachel and me a chance to talk.*

 **FIFTEEN**

"Oh dear, don't try to reach." From her seat across the table, Grandma Heinonen pushed the basket of rolls from the center of the table toward Emily. "We don't want you hurting yourself further."

Emily smiled, biting back a retort. She hadn't hurt herself on purpose, after all, but this was truly Grandma Heinonen's domain—the Blue Bonnet Bed and Breakfast—and she didn't want to be rude. The house itself was breathtaking: six thousand square feet, and every inch of it polished and shining. The kitchen was quirky, with chickens on the wallpaper border and china ones sitting on every shelf. Emily loved it all, but she most loved the story of the house.

Built by Captain Sarasin, the famous captain from Rock Harbor, so his wife could watch for his return, it was the last house on Houghton Street before it curved into Negaunee, the road out to the lighthouse Bree lived in. Emily could just picture the captain's wife out there, walking along the narrow widow's walk, staring out at Lake Superior, hoping to catch a glimpse of her husband's ship returning him to her. Sometimes those storms were big and scary. She wouldn't want to be out there during a nor'easter.

"Don't give any thought to what my mother said," Uncle Greg whispered from his seat beside Emily as he reached for the basket. He must have seen the stunned looked on her face.

Uncle Greg put a big pat of butter on a roll and set it on her bread plate, then continued whispering. "Did you know someone told Mom she looked like England's reigning monarch, Queen Elizabeth, and ever since, she's played up the resemblance as much as she can?"

Emily giggled behind her hand as she studied Grandma. Strands of silver highlighted her hair, mainly around her face. Dressed in a plaid-patterned dress with a soft skirt that swirled around just below her knees, she looked every inch the lady. Now that Uncle Greg mentioned it, yeah, Emily could see the resemblance to the pictures she'd seen of Queen Elizabeth.

Uncle Greg grinned. "Just ignore her. She doesn't mean anything by it. That's just the way she is." He nodded at her arm. "Does it hurt much?"

"A little." She glanced down at the crisscross rows. "The doctor said it'd probably leave a scar." Great—a constant reminder of her klutziness.

"I happen to think scars are very attractive on pretty young ladies." He smiled. "Proves you've had adventures."

"Really?" Then why was he dating a perfect model?

"Yep. Adds character."

"What adds character, Gregory?" Grandma finally turned from Dad and Naomi's conversation about Mayor Kaleva's reelection campaign.

"Life's little imperfections, Mother. Battle scars of survival."

Uncle Greg leaned closer to Emily. "I *am* a wild one like she said. But guess what, so is your dad."

Dad? Wild? Emily couldn't stop the snort.

"What? You don't believe me?"

Emily shook her head and took a sip of water. She couldn't picture Dad wild and crazy, and she had an overactive imagination, or so she'd been told.

"Back in high school, your dad was quite the charmer. Handsome. Star of the football team. Popular with the cheerleaders."

She swallowed. Her mother had been one of those cheerleaders.

"There were many nights we celebrated team victories well past curfews."

Dad . . . breaking curfew? Breaking any rule? She couldn't even picture him outside home or the hardware store. Out celebrating? Definitely not.

Uncle Greg nodded. "Several times." He shoved a bite into his mouth.

"You're pulling my leg."

"Nope. Truth." He held up two fingers. "Scout's honor."

"Emily, what's Greg lying about to you?" Dad stared down at them. "He was never a scout, just so you know."

Uncle Greg laughed. "You should know. You're the one who got me kicked out."

"I did no such thing." Dad smiled, a genuine smile like Emily hadn't seen in a long time.

Olivia's words came back to haunt her. Were Dad and Naomi having trouble like the Websters had?

"You did too, but I thank you for it. Profusely." He leaned next to Emily and spoke in a stage whisper, "I was never the scouting type. I'm not too good at improvising in a crisis situation."

"I don't know about that. You were always there to fix my problems." Naomi smiled at her brother.

"And I always will be." Uncle Greg smiled back. "That's what families are for. To stick together."

Emily noticed Dad's smile fall a bit. Was Uncle Greg trying to say he was here for Naomi because a divorce loomed on the horizon? Emily's throat tightened. She took another sip of water. This wasn't what she needed right now. She caught Timmy's confused look across the table. He didn't need this either. Naomi was the best thing that had ever happened to them. To think that she wouldn't be their stepmom anymore . . .

What was the scripture Pastor Lukkari talked about in this morning's sermon? Corinthians. Something about . . . *love never fails*. Yeah, that was it. Love never fails.

If love never failed, then why was there divorce? She didn't understand.

"Who wants a piece of pie?" Grandma stood, smoothing down her dress. She made the best pies this side of the peninsula—and she knew it. The whole town said they were the best.

"I'll help you." Naomi stood as well and gathered plates.

Emily couldn't lose Naomi. She just couldn't. If she had to, she'd just flat-out ask Naomi. Maybe if she made a plea on behalf of her and Timmy, Dad and Naomi could work everything out like Olivia's parents.

As Naomi smiled and handed her a piece of pie, Emily made up her mind. No matter what, she wouldn't lose Naomi. Not if she had anything to say about it.

The taste of pie still lingered on Emily's tongue, but it was mixed with fear. All the way home, she'd watched how quiet her dad and Naomi had been in the car. How Naomi had sat over against the door, staring into the dark night as if she had a million thoughts racing through her head. Emily fingered the stitches, which were still pulling at her skin.

Dad lifted a sleeping Matthew from the car seat and carried him indoors. Timmy walked sleepily after them while Emily trailed behind, wishing she knew how to bring up the subject. She absolutely, positively could *not* go to bed without knowing if their family was going to be split apart. She curled her fingers into her palms and went to the kitchen where she poured a glass of chocolate milk. She sipped at the milk while she listened to the sounds of Naomi and Dad putting Matthew and Timmy to bed.

Finally, her dad's footsteps came back toward the kitchen. He paused in the doorway. "Do your stitches hurt, honey? It's late. You should get ready for bed too."

The lump in her throat swelled until it pushed moisture into her eyes. At least that's what she told herself. She hated to cry. Biting her lip, she swallowed hard and blinked even harder. "I'm okay." Her voice came out in a half croak. "Did you know stitches were used in ancient Egypt?"

"News to me." He came closer. "Are you getting a cold?"

"No." Thank goodness Naomi's footsteps approached as well. Emily wanted them both in front of her when she asked *the question*. No way did she want to go through this more than once, and she'd be able to tell if they were trying to keep something from her.

"I was coming for some milk myself," Naomi said. Dark circles shadowed her eyes, and her hair was windblown. "Do you need a pain pill? The doctor told me what you could take." She poured herself a glass of chocolate milk.

"I'm fine!" The words came out a little more forcefully than Emily intended. "I mean, I need to talk to you both, but it's not about my cut."

Her dad and Naomi exchanged a long glance. "Sounds serious." Naomi carried her milk to the table and pulled out a chair. "Sit down and tell us what's wrong. You look like you're about to cry."

Even though Emily shook her head, the heat in her eyes intensified. She took a gulp of her milk and swallowed. "I never cry."

Her dad's lips twitched, and he nodded gravely. "Of course not." He sat beside Naomi and pulled out a chair for her. "Come over here and tell us what's wrong. Is it that boy—Josh?"

"It's much more serious than a stupid boy." And she wasn't about to tell him that she liked Brandon now anyway. Emily plopped onto the chair and took a deep breath. "Something is going on around here."

Naomi set her glass down. "What do you mean?"

"Do you think we haven't noticed how you guys are talking and then go quiet when we come into a room? Do you think we're too young to see how worried you are about something?"

*Tell me, please, just tell me.* She didn't want to have to say the ugly *D* word. It would be so much better if they voluntarily told her instead of leaving it to her to pull it out of them. Not that she was ready to face something so awful. Her lip trembled, and she bit down on it.

Her dad looked down at his hands, then back at Naomi, who

sagged against the back of the chair with a sigh. "I sometimes forget how grown up you are now," her dad said.

Naomi reached across the table and took Emily's hand. Emily clutched it and tried to steel herself for what was coming. The lump in her throat was growing to boulder size. "Are you getting a d-divorce?"

The awful word hung in the kitchen. Naomi's fingers tightened on Emily's hand. Her dad inhaled sharply. It was coming—the awful confirmation that their family was about to be torn apart.

Then her dad exhaled. "Of course not, Emily. Whatever gave you such a crazy notion? Naomi and I love each other very much. Divorce is never an option between me and Naomi. Put that idea right out of your head."

The air escaped Emily's lungs, and for one crazy second, she was sure she would burst into noisy sobs. She clutched Naomi's hand until the sensation passed. "Then what is it? And don't tell me it's nothing. Tell me the truth."

Naomi glanced at Emily's dad. "Donovan?"

Emily withdrew her hand from Naomi's grip and turned to her father. "You have to tell me." Could one of them be sick, like with cancer or something? The thought made her dizzy. One of her friends had lost her mom to ovarian cancer last year, and it had been so awful. "Are you sick?"

"No, honey, nothing like that," her dad said. He put his arm around her and pulled her against him so that her head rested on his shoulder. "I didn't want to worry you."

She pulled away. "Well, I'm worried, okay?"

"I can see that." He hesitated, and his gaze sought Naomi's again. "It's about your mother."

"What about her?"

Naomi nodded. "She's up for parole, Emily. In a week. But no one thinks she'll get out."

*Parole.* Emily gasped as the full realization hit. Her mother could get out, could come back for her and Timmy. Inetta had been right. "I don't want to see her. Ever! After she called, you promised I'd never have to talk to her again!"

"I'll do whatever I can to prevent her from coming around here," her dad said, his mouth grim. "The district attorney said we have a strong case after what she did."

"Strong but not for sure?" Emily sprang to her feet. "She nearly killed Timmy. You can't let her come here, Dad. Not ever."

"I'll protect you, Emily," he said.

She didn't doubt that he would try, but her mother was sneaky. And what would the other kids say if her mother came to town? Emily had barely been able to live down what had happened in the past. She couldn't go through that again.

Her eyes filled with tears, and she bolted for her room. Emily had one picture of her mother that she'd kept. Once she'd scrubbed every trace of tears from her face, she opened her sock drawer and pulled it out. The reason she liked it was because it showed the perfect family. Timmy with round cheeks, just a toddler, really. About three. Emily with her hair in pigtails and a gap-toothed smile. She'd just lost her first tooth. Her dad had his arm around her mother, who was smiling up at him with a happy expression.

It was all a lie, of course. Emily had no pleasant memories of growing up. Why did her mother even have to be considered for parole?

Life so wasn't fair.

 **SIXTEEN**

"I think he's way cuter than Josh," Emily said, smiling as she walked into the Monday afternoon sunshine. She'd spent the better part of the day trying not to think about her mother and parole. Olivia kept shaking her out of her worry by reminding her at least Dad and Naomi weren't getting a divorce. And neither had cancer. But still.

"Who's way cuter than Josh?" Olivia asked as she shrugged her arms through the straps of her backpack.

"Brandon Genrich, of course." Emily stared at the surf captain making his way to the gym.

On one hand, she was relieved to have a legitimate reason not to volunteer anymore—doing laundry and going out near Lake Superior were low down on her to-do list. But on the other hand, she wouldn't get to see Brandon anymore since they didn't have any classes together.

He gave Alex Hauglie a playful shove, then opened the gym door and let Alex enter first. Such a gentleman.

Emily smiled. "He's taller and stronger, and he's so nice. And did you know he's never missed being on Principal Sturgeon's 'All As' honor roll?"

"*Oooh,* really?" Olivia shook her head. "I think you're going boy-crazy, as my mom would say."

The blush crawled across Emily's cheeks, but she chuckled at Olivia. "Don't act like you don't go all mushy face when you talk to *Charles.*"

"Hey, you're the one who went from going all gooey over Josh Thorensen to all of a sudden goo-gooing over Brandon." But Olivia blushed and straightened. "Speaking of Charles, he told me that he'd pulled all he could on Mr. Lancaster."

"And?" Emily stopped about six feet from the gym where Brandon and Alex had disappeared just seconds ago for surf practice. "Did he find out anything else?"

"No, but I got to thinking . . ." Olivia tapped the end of her nose with her pointer finger like she always did when she was deep in thought. "Mr. Lancaster must handle a lot of money, right? Everybody knows models make a lot of money."

"Yeah, but he was fired for mishandling those clients' funds. Isn't that what the reports all said?"

"They did." Olivia nodded, still tapping the end of her nose. "But Mrs. Dancer's necklace is only worth about a thousand dollars. The round-trip airfare from Los Angeles to Rock Harbor is almost one thousand dollars alone. Doesn't make much sense for him to come all this way to steal a necklace that cost him half that to steal it."

Why did Olivia always have to use math to mark suspects off the list?

She stopped tapping her nose. "I don't know what he's doing here, and I do think he's kind of dishonest, but I don't believe he took the necklace."

Logic was a real theory buster.

Emily sighed. "Well, I'd still like to know how Valerie and Mr. Lancaster are connected. For Uncle Greg's sake."

"We'll keep looking until we figure it out." Olivia tugged Emily's backpack off her shoulder. "Now go and resign from your volunteer position."

The surf team was doing stretches in the gym. Emily quickly scanned the area for the coach, didn't see him, and so made for his office before anyone could make fun of her.

Brandon stood beside Coach Larson, who glanced up from the book they were studying when she gave a gentle knock on his office door. "Good, you're here. We have to get the new backup boards waxed and primed. I want the team to get them broken in during practices this week." Coach grabbed one of the bars of wax and held it out to her. "The backup boards are on the benches by the lockers."

Brandon smiled at her, nearly making her lose her train of thought and reason for being in the office. Coach's waving the bar of wax jerked her back into focus. "Uh, Coach, I'm going to have to resign from my volunteer position."

He frowned, making his nose appear even bigger. "Why's that? You don't seem like the quitting type."

Her face heated. "Th-thank you, Coach. I'm not." She held up her arm. "I had an accident Saturday night, and I needed stitches and I strained my other shoulder."

Brandon actually looked concerned, which made the heat in her face spread to her neck and chest.

"Were you in a car accident?" Coach asked.

"No, sir. I was taking part in a K-9 search-and-rescue call in the preserve at night. Brandon was there too. It was dark, and I lost my footing and fell."

Brandon was looking at her with admiration. Emily stood a little straighter. She hadn't had a chance to talk to him after she got back to park headquarters.

"*You* were part of a K-9 search and rescue?" the coach asked.

"Yes, sir. My stepmom, Naomi, works with Bree Matthews and Samson. Mrs. Matthews was unavailable, so the sheriff came to our house. Since it's a rule of the Kitchigami K-9 Search and Rescue team that no one goes out on an SAR alone, I got to go along and help with Charley. He's our SAR dog. Especially since I helped out at the training school this summer, and I'll be getting my own puppy to train soon and all." At least she hoped she was still getting that puppy.

"Well, well, well . . . I didn't realize we had a heroine in our midst." Coach nodded at her arm. "How bad?"

"Oh, four stitches, and my shoulder's strained. I'm not supposed to really do any lifting or anything with my arm for a week or so. At least until the stitches dissolve."

"I'm sorry to hear that. Sorry to lose you too." Coach Larson stood. "But I understand. You take care of yourself, okay? And come back as soon as you heal up."

"Thanks." She turned and headed back toward the gym. At least she could use the free time on her investigation or to study for the History Smackdown team. She was already a little behind for their next practice and needed to catch up on her flash cards.

Brandon fell in step alongside her. "You know, I think it's really cool that you help with the SAR. And that you were the one to find Rachel. You're really brave."

"Well, it was more of an accident than anything else." She smiled and tucked one of her crazy curls back behind her ear and giggled. "It doesn't take much bravery to fall down a hill and practically land on a lost person. I'm just glad we found her, thank God. I spent a lot of time praying for Rachel that night."

"I'm glad you're both okay." He walked with her across the gym, not even responding to some of the team's catcalls and whistles. "But seriously, it takes a lot of courage to go out in the dark to look for someone else. Especially in the Kitchigami Wilderness Preserve. That's where the Windigo lives, like we talked about."

Emily giggled. "I didn't see the Windigo the other night—did you?" She wouldn't dare admit to him that she'd been nervous thinking about the monster the whole time they'd been out. But she'd been in the woods, in the dark . . . it was only natural for her mind to play tricks on her.

"My people don't believe it's just an old story. Some of our elders have seen the Windigo in the woods. Mostly during the winter. That's when we need the most protection."

He had to be yanking her chain, teasing her to see if he could scare her. But Brandon didn't look like he was kidding, and he wasn't the type to scare someone for a joke.

"God is the provider of all protection, Brandon. Surely you know that?"

"You have your faith, and I have mine."

"But you believe in God, right?" She stopped just outside the gym door and peered into his chocolate-colored eyes. "And you don't really believe in the Windigo, do you?"

He paused, looking off in the distance toward Lake Superior. "Let's just say that I believe you can't have good without evil and that the world we live in is a balance between the two." He turned and headed back into the gym without another word.

What did *that* mean? She shuddered at the conviction she'd seen on his face. It seemed as though he had as much faith in the

Windigo as she had in God and Jesus. Could he have actually *seen* the Windigo?

The television blasted in the living room as Naomi quizzed Emily on her history with the flash cards. Every move made her shoulder hurt, and it was making Emily cranky.

But the television sounded louder than normal today. Timmy couldn't get enough of that stupid cartoon he had to watch. Every. Single. Day. It wore on Emily's last nerve. Or maybe she just needed another pain pill.

Naomi set the cards aside, then checked the chili in the slow cooker. "Timmy! Time to carry out the trash and wash up. You need to set the table."

"Aw. Can't I finish watching my show first?"

"No. Come on."

Emily's cell phone rang. Probably Olivia, but maybe she had some information on Mr. Lancaster. Emily dug it out of her pocket. "Hello?"

"Emily? It's Inetta."

"Oh, hi." She moved to the pantry. "What's up?"

"Listen, just wanted to give you a heads-up that we're going to run a follow-up on Mary Dancer. I'm on my way to interview her now."

"Really?" Emily thought Inetta was her friend.

"Yeah, she called Mr. Farmer and said the necklace was still missing and she didn't see much progress on the case from the sheriff, so she asked that we run a follow-up. I argued that I didn't think it was needed, but Mr. Farmer thought otherwise. He's sending a photographer too."

"I see. Thanks for letting me know." But she still was no further along on her suspects. All she'd managed to do was eliminate a few of them. The news article would just make everyone talk about her more.

"Why don't you come by the office after school tomorrow? Even if you can't give me a counter-interview, at least you'll know what's going in the paper before it hits."

Timmy ran down the hallway. Seemed like he had to run everywhere he went these days.

"Okay, thanks for letting me know. I've got to go. I'll see you tomorrow. Bye." She pushed the phone back into her pocket and stepped out of the pantry.

Naomi glanced at her. "Will you go put on the news so your dad can listen when he comes in and washes up?" She turned toward the bar stool where Matthew sat. "No, sir. You may not color on the counter."

Emily grinned and headed into the living room. She punched the button for the local news station and tossed the remote on top of one of Naomi's never-ending supply of books on the end table. She moved to head back to the kitchen when the reporter's words registered.

"Just an hour ago, a surfer on Lake Superior wiped out. According to eyewitnesses, his board hit him over the head, rendering him unconscious."

Emily froze. Fear of drowning kept her rooted to the spot, staring at the television.

The reporter standing outside the hospital continued, "Hospital staff has told us that the surfer is in critical condition here at Rock Harbor Hospital. This is Anula Grace, reporting live."

Emily closed her eyes as the image of the Superior's raging surf filled her mind, taking her back to another time. Her heart pounded as she pictured the water pushing against that poor surfer. Against her.

The lake was cold, but six-year-old Emily didn't mind. She shrieked when the waves hit her belly, then laughed and splashed Rachel.

Rachel screamed and ran back toward the sand. She scowled back at Emily, then went to her mother and pointed. Emily stuck her tongue into the hole where her tooth used to be. It hurt but felt good in a funny kind of way. She could just feel the edge of the new tooth coming in. Someday she would have beautiful white teeth like her mommy.

At the thought of her mother, she sought out a bright splash of red standing with two men. Daddy had met them here, but he'd started frowning when Mommy talked to the man in the blue swim trunks. Before Emily knew it, he'd had to go back to work. She waved at her mother, who didn't wave back.

A tight knot built in Emily's chest. Mommy never seemed to notice her. She fawned over Timmy sometimes, but the only time she said much to Emily was to tell her to watch out for her little brother. Out of habit, Emily's gaze went to where Timmy was building a sand castle with three other little kids. He was fine. She could enjoy herself. Waving at Rachel, she waded out into the waves until they were up to her chest.

It was so *cold*! Her teeth chattered a little, but she wasn't a baby. She even knew how to read a little now. And her daddy had taught her how to dog-paddle, so when the next wave passed, she kicked out her feet and dog-paddled a bit in the water.

"Look at me, Mommy!" she yelled above the waves, but her mother still paid no attention.

Maybe if she went out deeper and showed how big she was, Mommy would notice. She paddled a little farther out. What a good swimmer she was! Daddy would be impressed if he were here. She could swim clear out to the foghorn buoy all by herself. This swimming was easy. With a backward glance, she checked to make sure her mother wasn't smiling at her, then struck out toward the buoy. It wasn't that far.

She'd gone a few feet when a large wave came out of nowhere and caught her in the face. The cold water closed over her head, and she couldn't breathe. Which way was up? Where was the sky? She couldn't find it as she fought to get her head above the water. The wave churned her over sand along the bottom, and if she could have breathed, she would have cried at the pain in her arm and knee.

Just when she thought she would have to breathe or die, the wave tossed her to the top again. She sucked in a deep breath and began to cry weakly. Reaching out with one foot, she tried to touch bottom and couldn't. Her chest squeezed, and she tried to scream for her mother, but the wind snatched her cry away. Gulls cawed overhead as though mocking her.

All she had to do was dog-paddle back to shore. Daddy had taught her. She could do it. But when she looked at the shore, it was so far away that she began to cry harder. "Mommy!" Fear dragged at her limbs, and she found it hard to keep her head above water.

She swallowed another mouthful of water and tried again. She couldn't make it. She screamed the next time her head bobbed up over the water. "Help!"

A man sitting on the beach with his wife looked up and down

the beach, then out to the water. At first, he gazed about only five feet from the shore. She screamed again, and he saw her. He plunged into the water and swam toward her. Another wave hit her and propelled her to the sandy bottom again. She couldn't breathe, couldn't think past the cold water squeezing the life out of her. Her hands grasped fistfuls of sand. She needed to go up to where there was air.

Her lungs burned, and she struggled to figure out how to get her head above the water. Then fingers wrapped around the crisscross straps on the back of her swimsuit and yanked her up. She had to breathe—she had to. Unable to help herself, she inhaled and water burned its way into her lungs and nose. Then her head crested the water.

She was still choking and couldn't breathe. The next thing she knew, she was on the sand and water was pouring out of her nose and mouth. When she could finally breathe again, people were all around. She was so embarrassed she started to cry, but the man gathered her in his arms. She clung to him until her mother rushed toward her.

"Oh, my darling Emily. Are you okay?" Mommy pulled her from the man. She stood, holding Emily tight. "Are you all right, honey?" She grabbed Timmy's hand and led them toward the car, never even bothering to thank the man for pulling Emily out of the water.

Mommy put Timmy in his car seat, then helped Emily into the backseat. "You're okay, aren't you? You're Mommy's big girl, right?" She smiled and pushed the curls off Emily's forehead.

She loved that Mommy looked at her right now with all the attention she used to. "Yes, Mommy."

"Good. Good. That's my sweetheart. There's no reason for

Daddy to know about your little incident, right? We wouldn't want him to think you were still a baby and he shouldn't take you swimming anymore, would we? This can be our little secret." Mommy put her hands on her hips and stared at Emily. Then she smiled. "You won't tell Daddy our little secret, will you?"

"No, Mommy." She swallowed. She didn't care if Daddy ever took her anywhere near the water. She just wanted to be home in her bed and never put a toe in the lake ever again.

"Emily, what's wrong?" Naomi stood behind the couch. "Are you okay? You're white as a sheet."

She shuddered and forced the memory away. She stood slowly, her legs still weak under her weight. "A surfer wiped out and is in the hospital."

"Oh, mercy. I know how the water scares you." Naomi came and put a comforting arm around her shoulders.

Emily let Naomi's loving touch give her strength. She'd never told Dad the secret. Just kept it inside until it no longer mattered. But it did. She'd kept an important secret from Dad, all because her mother had manipulated her, just like she always did.

No matter if her mother made parole or whatever, Emily would never speak to her.

# SEVENTEEN

"I can't believe Mrs. Dancer called the paper and asked for a follow-up interview." Emily stomped down the street with Olivia. Thank goodness her shoulder was a little better today, because every time she'd rolled over on it last night, it had woken her up with pain. "It's like she wants the sheriff to arrest me or something."

Olivia chuckled. "I bet the sheriff would like this to be solved, Em. It's an election year. Mayor Kaleva has already started with her campaign calls and flyers. The sheriff is her husband, and if he can't get a big case like this solved, it might make her look bad." She gestured to the papers on the street post at the intersection of Jack Pine and Houghton. "Bet she'll use the surfing championship this weekend to campaign big-time."

Was the surfing championship really this weekend? Emily felt horrible for having to resign from the team with the championship so close. She could only pray someone else would step up and volunteer to help them.

"Maybe so, but I hope he isn't so pressured to solve the case that he just blames me based on what we know right now."

"I don't think Sheriff Kaleva would do that. He's got a pretty good reputation in town. I don't think he would judge so quickly."

Guilt formed a lump in Emily's throat. She'd been as judgmental as everyone else—immediately suspecting Mrs. Cooper just because the lady needed money to support her family. They were all wrong to jump to conclusions. Had she learned nothing in all the Bible studies she'd participated in over the years? She licked her lips.

"Hey, look." Emily grabbed Olivia's arm.

"What?"

"Is that Mr. Lancaster coming out of the inn?"

The small neon sign over the building across the street from the Suomi Café read ROCK HARBOR INN. Emily remembered learning about Rock Harbor's history in school. The building that was now the inn had been a French trading post in the town's glory days in the 1800s. A man who looked an awful lot like Mr. Lancaster stood just outside the inn's front door, looking up and down Houghton Street as if he were lost.

"That's him." Olivia gasped. "What's he doing?"

"I don't know. Looks like he's waiting on something."

"Should we follow him?" This could be a real lead, and she sure needed one with how fast she seemed to be scratching names off her list.

"Are you crazy?"

Before Emily could answer that, a dark car pulled up to the curb. Mr. Lancaster glanced around, then ducked into the backseat. The car roared off. "Guess we won't be following him anywhere. Did you recognize the car?"

Olivia ignored her, dropping her backpack to the ground and digging around inside.

"What are you doing?"

"Shh." She opened a notebook and jotted. Then she stood and smiled as she put everything into her pack and hoisted it over her shoulder. "I got the license plate number."

Impressive. "That's awesome, Liv, but, uh, what are you going to do with it?"

Excitement slid right off Olivia's face. "I don't know. People always get the license plate number in the movies and cop shows."

"Hey, it might come in handy. If he goes missing, you'll have something to give to the sheriff. Maybe that would help him solve the case."

They turned onto Pepin Street and entered the newspaper office within minutes. Inetta waited in the front for them. "I was beginning to think you had forgotten me."

"Of course not!" Emily said with a smile. Then she dumped her backpack on the floor and winced as it slid from her shoulder.

"What happened to you?"

Emily told Inetta the story.

"I'm glad you're okay! I really should interview you and your stepmom about that SAR. It'd give you some great public opinion."

Emily nodded. She probably needed it. "What did Mrs. Dancer say about me this time?"

"She didn't point the finger at you, at least not by name. She's offering a reward for the return of the missing necklace."

"Really?" Dad had made it sound like Mrs. Dancer needed the money from the sale of the necklace. If that were the case, she wouldn't have funds for any reward. "How much of a reward?"

"Five hundred."

That was a lot of money! "Wow."

"Yeah. Mary states, and I quote . . ." Inetta grabbed her

laptop and set it on the counter. She used the laptop's keypad and scrolled. "'My Sapphire Beauty is a one-of-a-kind necklace, with the special enchantment to keep the wearer safe from the clutches of the Windigo. The value, and the enchantment, are diminished if worn by someone who stole the necklace.' End quote."

"Do the Ojibwa really believe in the Windigo and charms of protection from it? It all seems so silly."

Inetta shrugged. "I don't know. She acted that way. Several of her family members were around during the interview, and they seemed serious enough about it." She took a sip of her coffee. "I'm serious about that interview with you and Naomi. How about I come by and talk with you both the day after tomorrow? After school? I'll bring a photographer. I'll call your dad and get permission."

"Sure. I guess if Dad says it's okay." A feature might also provide some free publicity for the SAR training center. That might help her get her puppy even though she didn't have enough money yet.

"Great. As you know, pictures make all the difference. I heard someone say that Mary's jewelry sold more after we ran our feature article on the festival that highlighted her."

Maybe that was how she could afford the reward money.

"We took more pictures of her and her jewelry today."

"Really?"

"Yeah. Look." Inetta turned her laptop toward Emily. "Just click the arrow at the top right of the screen to scroll through these pictures. Mr. Farmer hasn't decided which ones he'll use with the article." She pulled her iPhone from her pocket. "I'm going to call your dad, then set our interview in my calendar so I don't forget."

Emily stared at the first shot—Mrs. Dancer sitting behind a worktable, her beads and glass spread out. Another picture of Mrs. Dancer in front of a display. Probably wouldn't use that one as two little kids were in the shot, too much to be cropped out. They must've run through just as the photo was taken. They reminded Emily of Timmy and Dave.

She smiled and scrolled to the next photo. Another picture of Mrs. Dancer, this time beside a display of her Ojibwa-centered items. They truly were some of her most beautiful work. One day Emily hoped to be that good.

"There. I have the interview with you and Naomi set for Thursday around three forty-five. I told your dad I wanted to prove your innocence."

Emily nodded and started to scroll to the next picture, but stopped when she realized a person had been caught in this shot too. They could probably crop him out, though, as he was more in the background. Emily leaned closer to the laptop screen . . . There was something so familiar—

She sucked in air as she recognized the guy in the corner of the picture.

Brandon Genrich.

"What a crummy week." Emily flopped on the sofa beside Olivia and reached for her history flash cards. If only her stitches would heal as quickly as her shoulder had. "I'm tired of my arm hurting. And I *especially* wish I'd never asked my parents what was wrong. Now every time the phone rings, I think it's going to be my mother calling to say she's out of prison."

Naomi had fixed the girls a snack of cheese sticks and a

vegetable tray before taking Timmy and Matthew outside to play. She'd seemed excited about the highlighting of the Kitchigami Search-and-Rescue Training Center.

Emily fanned out her history cards, then reached for a cheese stick.

"Don't worry about your mom's parole," Olivia said. "You know your dad won't let her near you."

"I wish I could be certain."

"Did you tell Timmy?"

Emily nodded. "He was pretty upset, and I don't blame him. He has nightmares about her. Poor kid." Best not to say anything about *her* nightmares. "And we still aren't any closer to figuring out who took Mrs. Dancer's necklace. All we've managed to do is eliminate suspects."

A car door slammed outside.

"Dad must be home a little early."

Timmy shouted, and Matthew yelled for their dad. It was always chaos when their dad got home.

Emily shuddered. "Maybe we'd better go to my room."

She shut her book, and Olivia grabbed the tray of snacks. Emily hopped up as she heard the sound of the front door opening.

"Em?" her dad called from the entry.

"I'm in the living room," she hollered back.

"Come outside a minute. I have something to show you." He sounded excited.

Emily shrugged and put her book back on the coffee table. "I wonder what's going on?" She and Olivia went to join her dad on the porch. It wasn't often she heard that note in her father's voice. He was usually laid-back.

No one was on the porch when they stepped outside in the

crisp fall air. The scent of turning leaves hung in the air. "What's up, Dad?"

Her dad was by the porch with the rest of the family. Bree and Samson were there as well. Naomi stood with her back to the door and both of Emily's brothers were in front of her. They seemed to be looking at something she was holding. Samson had his front paws on Naomi's leg.

"What's going on, Dad?" Emily couldn't see what Naomi had in her arms.

His smile grew bigger. "Naomi and I have something for you. You've had a rough few weeks, and we wanted to do something to cheer you up."

Her heart thumped. A present for her? What could it be? A new iPod? Or maybe even a laptop? She dismissed that idea. Her dad didn't have the money to buy an expensive laptop.

"Turn around, Naomi," her dad said.

When Naomi turned around, she was smiling hugely. A golden brown fur ball was in her arms.

Emily gaped, unsure of what she was seeing. "Daddy!" she squealed. "Is this *my* puppy?" She leaped toward Naomi and hesitantly touched the top of the puppy's head. "He's so soft."

Naomi deposited the soft, warm body into Emily's arms. Emily kissed the top of his head. "He's adorable. I thought you weren't going to let me have him!"

"Emily, I owe you an apology. I'm not proud that I didn't automatically believe you when you said you weren't lying. I should have given you the benefit of the doubt. You're my daughter, and you've never lied to me before. I know you didn't steal that necklace. And you would have had the money to pay for him if this necklace business hadn't happened. I'm sorry." Her father's eyes crinkled when he smiled again. "I'm really proud of what a responsible young woman you are becoming. What are you going to call him?"

"Thanks, Dad," Emily said, tears welling up in her eyes. It felt really good to know her dad was on her side. She gave him a quick hug, trying not to squish her new puppy in the process. "I guess I'd better decide on a name. I haven't thought much about it because I thought it would be ages before I got him." She studied the soft golden fur and bright eyes. "How about Sherlock? He's going to be a great search dog, just like Sherlock was a great detective."

"I love it!" Olivia rubbed the puppy's head.

"He was ready for his new home," Bree said. "I haven't had much time to spend with him, and all his siblings are gone. He needs a little pampering."

"I'll give it to him." Emily felt something warm on her hand and grimaced when she realized he'd wet on her. "Uh-oh, looks like he got a little excited." She hugged him again. "But I'll wash."

Timmy danced around her. "Can I hold him?"

Naomi shook her head. "Now, Timmy, your sister just got him. There will be plenty of time for you to hold him later. Let's let Emily enjoy her first night without being pestered."

Emily shot her a thankful grin. "Can we get him a collar?"

Her dad produced a blue collar from his pocket. "Already taken care of. I got one in your favorite color." He fastened it around the dog's neck. "Very handsome, Sherlock."

The bright blue strap had a star on it, and it appeared to be good-quality leather. She didn't even want to think about how much money they'd spent on the puppy.

She handed the dog to Timmy and threw her arms around her dad again, then hugged Naomi as well. "You guys are the *best*!

Now I have to get him trained so he can be as good as Charley and Samson someday."

Samson's ears flicked up at the mention of his name. He touched Sherlock's nose as if he was making sure the little ball of fur was up to his standards.

Emily took her dog back and patted Samson's head. "I know there's no dog like you, boy, but I'll work hard and make you proud of him."

And she'd work hard to find who stole Mrs. Dancer's necklace to make sure her dad stayed proud of her.

 **EIGHTEEN**

"Isn't he so smart?" Emily asked Olivia as she beamed down at Sherlock, who'd taken to being walked on a leash very well.

They reached the corner of Cottage Avenue and Houghton Street, and took a left toward Emily's dad's hardware store. The wind picked up, and the smell of the lake carried over the air. The weather forecaster said a front might move through tonight, bringing rain, but that everything should clear up tomorrow midmorning and stay clear through the surfing championship on Saturday.

"Emily! Emily!"

Olivia nudged her, bringing her from her thoughts. Emily spun to see Brandon sprinting in her direction. Her breathing hiccupped, but she couldn't help but think of him in that picture of Inetta's. What had he been doing at Mrs. Dancer's?

"Hey." He drew to a stop in front of her.

"Hi, Brandon." Her tongue felt thicker than usual. "Uh, do you know Olivia? Olivia Webster."

He smiled and shook Olivia's hand. "Brandon Genrich, nice to meet you." He turned his attention to the puppy. "Is this your dog?"

"Yeah. I just got him."

"What's his name?"

"Sherlock."

"Like the detective?" He grinned. "That's cool."

"Yeah." She couldn't bring herself to ask him about the picture. What was she supposed to do, just blurt it out?

"I think I just saw a picture of you." Olivia helped her out.

"You did?" Brandon smiled. "Doing what?"

"You were just in a shot the newspaper took of Mary Dancer."

He nodded. "That's my aunt. My mom's sister."

"I didn't know that," Emily said. "I mean, not that I should or anything, but I just didn't." Oh, she sounded so lame. She bent to rub Sherlock's silky coat. That made her feel better.

"Yeah. I help her out in her shop sometimes. Sweeping the floor. Cleaning out cases."

Emily's chest tightened as she straightened. "So that's why you believe in the Windigo? You're Ojibwa?"

Under his darker complexion, he blushed. "Well, sure. We all know there are things we can't explain in the woods."

Heat snaked up the back of Emily's neck. "I don't think there are monsters in the woods."

"I do." His Adam's apple bobbed as he swallowed. "It pays to be careful, Emily. All of us should be on our toes." He glanced over his shoulder toward the community center. "Well, I'd better get back to helping Mr. Zinn with moving some boxes, then head home. I have to help my uncle with preparations for the sweat lodge."

"S-sure," Emily stammered.

"I'll see you around." Brandon smiled at Olivia. "You too, Olivia."

"See you around."

He flashed another of his shining smiles at Emily, then jogged back across the street.

"Wow, he *is* cute," Olivia breathed. "I've never been this close to him before."

Emily giggled. "I know, right?" She nudged her best friend. "Hey, he's not Charles."

Olivia blushed. "I've got to get home. I told Mom I'd help with dinner, so we'd better hurry."

Emily led Sherlock at a fast pace alongside her best friend, but her mind stayed on Brandon. Mary Dancer was his aunt. She believed Emily had taken her necklace and had all but flat-out accused her to the sheriff. But Brandon believed in her.

Wow.

Emily rushed into the house, the puppy's paws skidding on the wood floor. She flung herself to her knees and laughed when he nibbled on her chin. "Good boy," she crooned.

Naomi came from the kitchen with a towel in her hands and Matthew hanging on to her jeans. "He was so rambunctious all day. I think he missed you. Taking him for walks on a leash is really good for him."

"I just love him so much. Thank you again, Naomi. For everything." Tears filled her eyes, and Emily had to blink not to cry. She stood, holding her puppy against her chest.

Naomi smiled and gave her a quick hug. Sherlock protested the confinement by nipping at Emily's chin again.

She laughed, the unshed tears disappearing. "Is he hungry?"

"I doubt it. I was bad and gave him a few pieces of meat from the roast I'm fixing before you took him out."

Emily kissed the top of his head and set him back on the floor. "Would you help me start training him—just until I can get the money to put him in the school?"

Naomi's eyes softened. "Of course, honey. We can start with basic stuff, but you'll need to get him in school to get used to the different aspects of a search." She glanced back into the kitchen. "We've got a few minutes. Let's go outside. Matthew, you want to hide from the puppy?"

Emily's little brother giggled and nodded. "He won't find me!"

"I'll grab a paper bag and one of Matthew's dirty socks."

Naomi was so terrific. Emily took Matthew's hand and led him out to the porch. She left the puppy on the porch and pointed out some good hiding spots. "Don't let me see where you hide."

Emily turned to avoid seeing where he was hiding as Naomi came onto the porch with a sack in her hand. She opened the sack. "Let him sniff it," Naomi said.

Emily put the puppy on the porch floor and held him still while Naomi held the open bag under the puppy's nose. Sherlock sniffed around the bag but didn't put his nose inside. "Here, inside the bag." Naomi opened the mouth of the sack wider and thrust his nose against the sock. The pup sniffed eagerly.

"I'm ready," Matthew called, his voice over near the swing set.

Emily carried Sherlock down the steps and set him in the yard. "Find Matthew, boy." She offered him another whiff of the sock. Better him than her. Matthew's dirty socks did not smell good!

He took off toward the woods at the side of the property. "Not that way," she called, laughing. "This is hard."

"He'll get the hang of it," Naomi said. "Everything smells new and exciting right now." She shaded her eyes with her hand. "Looks like Mason is here."

Emily's gut tightened at the news. What was the sheriff doing? The white SUV had the sheriff emblem on it, so this wasn't a social call. Sherlock ran to meet this new playmate, and Sheriff Kaleva paused to rumple the puppy's fur.

He looked up and saw Emily watching him. "Afternoon, Em. I thought you'd be home by now. You and Naomi got a minute?"

"Sure," Naomi said. "Come on in and I'll pour you some coffee, Mason."

"I wouldn't say no."

"Em, would you fetch Matthew?"

The sheriff followed Naomi to the house with Sherlock chasing his boots. Emily was only too glad to go get her baby brother. The longer she could delay being hauled off to jail, the better.

Her mouth was dry when she grabbed a protesting Matthew and herded him inside. She found the sheriff and Naomi in the kitchen at the table with cups of coffee. They fell silent when she and Matthew entered. Not a good sign. Emily felt sick as she sat in the chair beside Naomi. Surely she wouldn't let the sheriff take her?

"Matthew, go watch cartoons with Timmy," Naomi said. "Timmy has some snacks."

"Okay." Matthew grinned and ran off toward the distant voice of Donald Duck.

Emily put her hands on the table. She might as well get this over with. "Are you going to arrest me?"

"Emily, the very idea!" Naomi said. "Of course not."

Sheriff Kaleva cleared his throat. "I wanted to see if you've heard anything around town about the theft. A little birdie told me you'd been poking into things."

He didn't seem too mad about it, so Emily gave a cautious nod. "We had a few suspects we've checked out."

"We?" Naomi asked, frowning.

"Me and Olivia. Well, Timmy and Dave too." She didn't want to accuse the sheriff of not investigating so she shut up.

"And what have you found out?" he prodded. "What suspects?"

She couldn't tell him about her uncle, not with Naomi sitting right there. "Malia Spencer for one. But it's not her. A-and, well, Mrs. Cooper. But she's clean too."

Naomi gave a start. "Lucy? Good heavens, Emily, why would you suspect her?"

Emily's face burned, and she looked away from the shock in Naomi's face. "Well, she kind of needs the money, right?" She straightened. "And speaking of money, Mrs. Dancer has offered a five-hundred-dollar reward for the necklace's return."

"She must really want it back," the sheriff said. "I wish I'd been able to find it already." His piercing gaze landed on Emily. "For more reasons than one."

Emily held on to the compassion in his face. Maybe he wanted her to be innocent. She managed a smile. "Then there's Mrs. Dancer herself. Until she offered the reward, I'd thought she might have done it for the attention. You know, like people who claim to have won the lottery so they can get lots of interviews. Publicity could only help her business. But she's not going to offer a reward if she took it herself."

"True," the sheriff said, his lips twitching. "Is that it?"

"I guess so," she said. Other than her uncle, Mr. Lancaster, and Valerie. They weren't cleared yet.

Because if Uncle Greg wasn't here to be with his sister because of a divorce or marriage problems, why was he here?

She glanced at Naomi and wished she could voice her suspicions, but there was no way she was going to accuse Naomi's brother right in front of her.

At least not unless she had evidence.

 **NINETEEN**

Emily eyed the familiar blue car as Naomi maneuvered the SUV into a parking space. Inetta was already here. She licked her lips and swallowed. Why had she ever agreed to this interview?

Carrying Sherlock, Emily followed Naomi and Charley to join the dogs and people in the yard with Bree and Inetta. With any luck, there would be better people to interview than her. Her puppy squirmed to be let down, so she put him on the ground and he ran to touch noses with Samson.

Bree was dressed in jeans and a green sweater that looked great with her reddish hair and green eyes. Her smile broadened when Sherlock came over to lick her shoe. "I think he remembers me. Naomi tells me you've been doing some preliminary training with him."

Emily's face burned when everyone turned to look at her. "A little. He doesn't understand it yet."

"The other dogs will train him better than you can." Bree began to organize the collection of people and dogs.

Inetta stepped over to talk to Emily. "Thanks for helping me get this interview. I think my readers will be very interested, and one of the bigger papers might even pick it up." Her eyes were shining. "I'll get to see dogs being trained from puppies right up to seeing the master Samson at work."

"He's pretty awesome. Charley too," Emily said. "Uh, if you want to interview Naomi first, go ahead."

Inetta took out her pen and paper. "Let's start with you, Emily. What made you want to do search and rescue? It's not a normal activity for a teenager."

"I've been around it since my dad married Naomi, and when Timmy and I were lost in the woods, Samson found us. I knew right then I wanted to be part of something that awesome. I like helping people." She blushed at how silly her words sounded, but Inetta just smiled and nodded. Maybe she didn't sound as stupid as she felt. "That's why I've got to find that necklace. I'll get the money I gave to Mrs. Dancer back, and it will pay for my puppy, Sherlock's, training."

Bree approached and heard her words. "You know I wouldn't charge you to train Sherlock, Em."

"You know my dad. He won't let you train him if I don't pay for it. And really, he's right. When you pay for something, you value it more."

Bree patted her shoulder. "You're turning into quite the young lady, honey. I'm proud of you." She glanced at Inetta. "We're ready to start the training."

"My photographer is set up and ready. I can't wait." Inetta followed her.

"Let's go!" Bree shouted.

The rest of the students took the dogs around the building. Naomi got in what Emily had been told was a scratch box, a rough wooden box with a guillotine-type door. Emily shuddered when Bree dropped the door into position. She was glad *she* wasn't the one in the cage. Carrying a bag with the scent article of Naomi's for Bree, she followed her around the corner.

Emily never got tired of watching the dogs work. Bree lined up the dogs and handlers, then let the animals smell the scent article. The handlers began to release each dog individually and see how long it took them to find Naomi in the box.

Samson was the fastest to find Naomi, of course. He drove straight for the scratch box, jumping up on it and barking. He grabbed a stick off the ground and carried it to Bree with his tail held high in triumph. Bree praised him, rubbing his ears, and Emily patted him as well. She just loved that dog. Not as much as Sherlock, of course, but awfully close.

Each of the dogs got their chance. Sherlock took the longest, nosing around the meadow for nearly fifteen minutes before Bree turned Samson out to help him. The older dog quickly led the puppy to the box.

"Good dog," Naomi said, rubbing the puppy's head. "One of these days Emily and Sherlock will be as famous as Bree and Samson."

Bree smiled, and the approval on her face warmed Emily clear to her toes. She wanted to be just like Bree when she grew up.

They repeated the training exercise, then moved on to one in the woods. When the time was up, Emily was more tired than she'd expected, but at least Sherlock was beginning to get the gist of what he was supposed to be doing.

"That's it," Bree said. "I'll see you all on Saturday."

"Bree, could I ask you a few more questions?" Inetta asked. "Naomi and Emily too."

"Of course." Bree led her toward the building, and they entered the SAR center.

Inside the building, Bree moved over by the window and settled on the floor beside Samson cross-legged. Samson yawned, then moved over to plop his head on her lap. She absently played with his ears, and the dog gave a sigh of contentment. She picked up a brush and began to work it through the burrs in his coat. "What can I help you with?"

"I asked Emily why she wanted to be part of a search-and-rescue team, and she told me about you two rescuing her and Timmy. I'd forgotten all about that." She turned to Naomi. "And then you married Donovan and became her stepmom. It's such a heartwarming story. I'd like to do a feature on how events can be so interconnected. How you follow your dream and find a delightful surprise. And how that one event changed so many things—this center was started, other lives have been saved, and now Emily here is following in your footsteps."

Naomi's eyes widened. "Really? I've always thought our romance should be in a book. Oh, Donovan will laugh at this."

Emily nearly groaned. She was going to be the laughingstock of school when this article came out. She should have kept her mouth shut.

"I'm so glad to see everyone out this evening." Mrs. McDonald, their grandma's friend, had made a beeline for their table just moments after Naomi got Matthew situated in his seat at the new restaurant out on the M-18 highway.

Emily sat between Dad and Matthew and Timmy sat between Dad and Naomi at a round table. They'd never been to the restaurant before, but Dad had wanted to take everyone out to celebrate the great interview. He now bragged to Mrs. McDonald about his "girls." Emily looked around the new place as she tried not to blush, even though she loved having Dad's approval.

The building reminded Emily of pictures she'd seen of hunting lodges with big half logs for walls that were decorated with dream catchers made by the local Ojibwa tribe members. Several wampum belts hung on display from wooden pegs. She couldn't help but wonder what Brandon would think about the place.

The waitress came to the table and took everyone's drink orders and left menus for them to look over.

"I must let you enjoy your meal." Mrs. McDonald patted Naomi's shoulder. "I was supposed to meet your mother here, but she had to cancel at the last minute." She smiled. "So now I'm on my own."

"If you're here by yourself, why don't you join us?" Naomi asked.

"Oh dear, I couldn't intrude." But Mrs. McDonald's expression said the opposite.

"It's no intrusion. Really. Do come join us." Naomi's smile looked genuine.

"Well, if you insist. I'll just grab my purse and be right back."

"I'm sorry," Naomi whispered to Dad as Mrs. McDonald rushed to the other side of the restaurant. "I just couldn't stand for her to eat all alone."

Dad grinned. "Your generosity is one of the reasons I love you so much."

Timmy made gagging sounds while Matthew laughed. Emily laughed and scooted her chair closer to Dad's, making room for a place between her and Matthew. "She can sit by me." When her dad smiled with approval, she knew she'd done the right thing. And besides, if she could get Mrs. McDonald to talk, she might learn something about who took the necklace.

Mrs. McDonald returned and sat down on the seat next to Emily just as the waitress came and took their order. Once the waitress had left, Mrs. McDonald turned to Emily.

"How are you, dear? Your grandmother told me about your injury," Mrs. McDonald said as she pointed at Emily's arm. "Are you doing well?"

"It's fine." Emily would rather not talk about how clumsy she'd been.

Mrs. McDonald nodded. "Well, I'm glad you're okay. Naomi, I suppose you're happy your brother is here visiting."

Naomi smiled. "Very much so. I can't believe Mom finally got him to come. He usually stays away so that Mom can't try to convince him to move back here."

"She's been after him for years, dear. Years."

So his showing up wasn't sudden or surprising? Why hadn't Naomi mentioned it?

Naomi squeezed lemon in her tea. "I know. I hope Mom isn't too disappointed when he goes. He'll leave on Tuesday. He starts his new job the following Monday."

Uncle Greg was leaving on Tuesday? And he had a new job?

"Your mom said he took a position at a new company. I understand it's quite a prestigious promotion."

The waitress returned with their meals. After she left, Dad asked a blessing over the food, then Mrs. McDonald returned to the conversation. "I'm just pleased he came to visit your mother before he started his new position. It's made her quite happy."

"It has," said Naomi in between cutting Matthew's food and trying to grab a bite for herself.

"What about Valerie?" Emily couldn't believe she'd blurted that out loud.

Naomi gave Timmy a spoon for his soup. "What about her?"

"Isn't she with Uncle Greg?" The familiar burn lit her cheeks. "I mean, like boyfriend-girlfriend."

Dad threw back his head and laughed. "Oh, Em."

Naomi and Mrs. McDonald snickered.

She hated to be laughed at. "What?"

"Your Grandma Heinonen set Uncle Greg up with Valerie." Dad took a long swig of water. "She didn't wait long to start her matchmaking efforts."

"Mom thought she could entice Greg to stay in Rock Harbor if a beautiful woman turned his head. What better woman to do that than Valerie, who'd recently been named the spokesmodel for a bathing suit company?"

"Hey, a beautiful woman can make a man do things he never thought he'd do." Dad leaned over Timmy and kissed Naomi's cheek.

"Well, that's good, because we saw Valerie at the festival with a man. He's her manager, Kenneth Lancaster, who is probably a criminal." It felt good to let that out.

Naomi set down her water glass. "More investigating, Em?" Her brow creased with worry.

She shrugged with her uninjured shoulder. "He and Valerie were at our booths when Mrs. Dancer was in the bathroom. We sold him a necklace that she picked out."

"Why didn't you say anything to Sheriff Kaleva?" Dad asked.

"Because we didn't know who he was then. We just found out."

"How's that, dear?" Mrs. McDonald asked.

"We did some Internet research." Emily met Naomi's stare, then dropped her gaze into her lap. "He's been fired by several models for *mishandling* funds." She lifted her eyes. "But there's no logical reason for him to be here in Rock Harbor unless he's with Valerie. And if he's with Valerie, then that was bad for Uncle Greg."

Mrs. McDonald dabbed her mouth with her napkin. "Oh my. I can help you with that mystery. Mr. Lancaster is staying at the inn, and you all know Patty Solka, the manager, is my friend. Anyway, she said Mr. Lancaster has been dating Valerie's older sister."

*Wow.* So Mr. Lancaster was dating Valerie's sister.

"If memory serves me correctly, I believe Valerie mentioned something about picking out a gift for her sister's birthday at the festival." Mrs. McDonald folded her napkin and laid it across her plate.

Well . . . that made sense. But why had Valerie acted so strangely when Emily mentioned she'd seen her? Was it because she'd been with her manager, who was a thief? Did she know that? She had to. Maybe she couldn't fire him because he'd break her sister's heart.

Matthew spilled his milk in his lap. Dad grabbed him while Naomi reached for the glass.

"I'll take this little man to get cleaned up," Dad said and headed toward the bathroom, Matthew in his arms.

Naomi threw napkins on the spill, sopping up the milk.

"I heard Mary Dancer has put up a reward for the return of her necklace," Mrs. McDonald whispered to Emily.

"I heard that too," Emily whispered back.

"I wonder if Mason has received any tips?" Mrs. McDonald handed her napkin to Naomi, then turned back to Emily. "Have you heard of any?"

"No, ma'am." But maybe that's what his visit yesterday was all about. Feeling her out, seeing what she knew.

Her gut knotted. What if he thought she was guilty and told her about the reward just so she'd be tempted to "find" the necklace to get the reward money? Had he come by just to feel her out about it?

"I also heard Mary's family is very interested in getting the necklace back. It had apparently been made with the beads that had been 'blessed' with the tribe's medicine man equivalent, so it is believed to have serious protective and preventive power. They weren't very happy she was selling it."

*Hmm.* Maybe she could ask Brandon about who in their family wanted that necklace back and if any were serious enough to take it.

"Do you believe that?" Emily whispered. "That such a blessing could give something power like that?"

"Of course not, dear. I believe in God and his Son, Jesus, and the power of the Holy Spirit. That's all the protection I need."

Very true.

Mrs. McDonald peered down her nose at Emily. "You don't believe it either, do you?"

"No, ma'am."

"Good. I'd hate for you to fall prey to such nonsense."

 **TWENTY**

"Have you heard the news?" Olivia shoved off the lockers as soon as Emily entered the school's hallway.

"They found the necklace?" This could so be the answer to her prayers. She held her breath as she slumped her backpack to the floor.

Olivia frowned. "No. I'm sorry. I meant about the surfing championship."

Emily reached for her lock and rolled the dial for the combination. "It's okay." She let out a disappointed sigh. She should've known better. If the necklace had been found, surely the sheriff would have called Naomi and Dad.

The bell rang, and the girls went to their different homerooms. Mrs. Harris stood at the front of Emily's class. "Principal Sturgeon is asking all students to make encouragement cards for the surfing team for their championship meet this weekend. They'll be distributed among the team members. So put away your books." She gestured to the two boxes on the table in front of the first row of desks. "Please take one of the blank cards and an envelope from one box, and markers and stickers from the other. Feel free to decorate your card however you wish."

Students murmured to one another as everyone made their way to the front of the room to grab supplies. Rachel Zinn moved beside Emily, who waited behind the groups crowding around the boxes.

"Hi, Emily. How're you doing?"

"Good."

"Hey, did you hear about Mrs. Dancer putting up a reward for the return of her missing necklace?"

"Yeah." Emily hadn't quite gotten comfortable with the change in her and Rachel's relationship. Ever since their truce had been called, Rachel had been friendly, but Emily didn't know if she could trust that. After all, she and Rachel had been friends since childhood, only to have Rachel turn on her for something Emily had no control over. Would she do it again? Emily was hesitant to let her guard totally down.

"Did you know the bank's been threatening to take her house because she can't make her payments?"

Emily stopped moving forward with the group and faced Rachel. "I didn't know that. How do you?"

Rachel's face turned bright red. "Well, my punishment for running away is to help out at my dad's fishing resort. Answering the phone, filing . . . stuff like that. I was in the office filing receipts yesterday when I heard Dad and Mr. Kukkari talking."

"He's running for mayor, right?"

"Yeah. He came by to ask Dad for a campaign contribution." Rachel glanced at Mrs. Harris, who sat engrossed in whatever was on her computer monitor. "Anyway, Mr. Kukkari was appealing to Dad's business sense, I guess. Saying how Mayor Kaleva had gotten soft and that she was making business decisions based on emotions, not logic."

"What does that have to do with Mrs. Dancer?"

"Give me a second." Rachel smiled. "He said something about her making a recommendation to the bank to give certain Rock Harbor people longer to pay their house notes. He said that the bank could take homes and sell them for a profit, and someone else could buy and flip them, or something."

That sounded cold. Banks could just do that?

"Dad asked him for an example, and Mr. Kukkari said people like Mrs. Dancer, who didn't even have a *real* job with no means of a paycheck."

"Girls, come on." Mrs. Harris stood and stared.

Emily had been so engrossed in Rachel's story that she hadn't noticed there was no longer a line at the boxes and everyone except her and Rachel had returned to their seats and were working on cards. She grabbed a blank card and envelope, two markers, and a couple of sheets of stickers and rushed back to her desk.

But her mind wasn't on creating a card. If Mrs. Dancer couldn't pay her house payment, how would she pay a reward for the return of her necklace?

Emily absolutely adored being in Bree and Kade's lighthouse. She loved the age of it, the way the wood floors squeaked when she stepped on them, and the way the sun slanted through the wavy glass in the windows.

"This is such a cool house," Olivia said as they finished putting the dinner dishes into the dishwasher.

"I love lighthouses. I'd like to see the Tower of Hercules. It's a Roman lighthouse in Spain." She sighed. "I love Roman history."

Olivia wrinkled her nose. "You like all history."

Hannah, one of Bree's three-year-old twins, tugged at Emily's leg. "I want to swing." Her twinkling eyes tugged at Emily's heart.

"Okay." Emily allowed herself to be pulled toward the door. Hunter ran to join them too. "Just for a bit, though. It's almost time for your baths." And bed, but Emily didn't want the wailing to start.

"Thanks for helping out this afternoon, girls," Bree called after them.

"You're welcome," Emily and Olivia said in chorus.

Bree had asked them to keep the children entertained while she got the house ready for company. Dave was with Kade, so they just had the twins to take care of. Samson, trailed by Emily's adoring puppy, followed them outside. He rarely let the children out of his watchful sight, and Sherlock never let the big search dog out of *his* sight. That was fine with Emily. Maybe her puppy would pick up some of Samson's expertise.

They put the children in the swings and began to push them. Samson lay down on the ground, and Sherlock curled up by his belly. So cute. Emily yanked her cell phone from her pocket and snapped a picture. Lightning flashed high overhead. Emily glanced at the darkening sky and winced at Olivia. "We'd better get them inside. The storm's coming fast." As was common in Rock Harbor, storms could build and erupt without much notice.

Samson lifted his head and gazed toward the house. Moments later Bree charged through the door with his search vest and backpack in her hand. "Samson, come!"

"Wait here," Emily told Olivia, who worked to get Hannah out of her swing.

Emily ran to join Bree. "What's wrong?"

Bree was white. "The Coopers were having a picnic, and Mrs. Cooper's daughter, Pansy, wandered into the woods while Lucy was taking stuff out of the car." She knelt to slip the search vest on her dog.

"Oh no! Naomi was taking Timmy to a movie after his doctor appointment. I could get Charley and help. Olivia could stay with the twins." She didn't like that Pansy was missing, but she'd love the chance to go out on another SAR.

Bree considered the offer. Emily could tell that she didn't want to risk Emily getting hurt again on a rescue, but she finally nodded. "We need all the help we can get with the storm coming up. I have two on my team I can call, but Charley is one of our better dogs. Let me make sure your dad doesn't mind." She pulled her cell phone out and dialed.

"I'm sure he won't mind. I'll tell Olivia." While Bree made the call, Emily ran to tell Olivia what was going on. Emily helped get Hunter out of the swing too and handed him off to her best friend. Olivia promised to pray for them while she watched the twins and Sherlock.

"Your dad says it's okay," Bree said when Emily returned. "We'll stop and get Charley on the way."

They piled into Bree's SUV. A few minutes later, both Samson and Charley were securely contained in their crates, and they were on their way to the forest.

The storm front pushed out the bright autumn weather and replaced it with a cold drizzle as they drove toward the park.

"It's going to be cold and wet," Emily said. "Will that make it harder to find Pansy?" Not to mention that it'd be dark soon.

"No, the dogs will love it. The moisture in the air will help them." Bree pulled into the parking lot next to the picnic area and turned off the vehicle.

Emily jumped to the ground and went to let the dogs out. None of the other team members were there yet, but other searchers milled around the area. Emily's cheeks heated when she recognized Brandon pushing aside branches and calling for Pansy. What was he doing here?

Mrs. Cooper saw them coming and rushed toward them. Slender with fine blond hair and green eyes, she looked frantic. "You've got to find her, Bree."

Her face was wet, and it wasn't from the rain. Samson whined and pressed against her leg as if to offer comfort. She dropped to her knees and buried her face in his fur.

Bree put her hand on Mrs. Cooper's shoulder. "We'll find her. Any sign of her at all?"

Mrs. Cooper shook her head. "Some of the Ojibwa who were here for a tribal picnic have been helping me look, but they won't stay once the sun goes down. They say that the Windigo lives here and prowls after dark."

Emily straightened. The Windigo lived in this particular section of woods? The news made her shiver, despite her not believing the legend. Brandon's convictions gave her the willies.

"Do you have a scent article?" Bree asked Mrs. Cooper.

Mrs. Cooper raised her head and nodded. "I'll get it. I've got a paper sack to put it in."

The rest of the team began to arrive while they waited for Mrs. Cooper to return. Brandon came toward Emily. "You're here to search for the kid?"

She nodded, suddenly tongue-tied.

"Me too."

"You're not afraid? I heard some of your people wouldn't search here after dark because of the Windigo." Emily could have bitten off her tongue. Had she just insulted him and his heritage?

He shrugged. "I'm perfectly safe. Can I come with you and your dog?"

Interesting, since he'd said just days ago that he believed in the Windigo. Why wasn't he worried? Had he just been messing with her before? "Uh, sure."

Mrs. Cooper returned with the bag. Once she had the search article, Bree sent her team out to search the area. With Charley on a lead, Emily and Brandon followed her and Samson into the open field next to the house. Emily glanced at the darkening sky and winced. The storm clouds obscured what little daylight remained and made the interior of the forest even darker.

Bree must have noticed because she nodded. "Hypothermia sets in quickly in these conditions. An added problem is the thickness of the forest. The trees are so close together it's hard to walk through it."

The dogs sniffed the scent article, a jacket Mrs. Cooper had put in the paper sack. Samson sniffed the bag and began to wag his tail. Bree let him off his leash. He crisscrossed the field with his nose in the air then headed toward the woods across the road.

"He's got her scent!" Bree took off after him.

Charley tugged away from Emily and whined. She released him from his leash, and he raced after Samson. Emily jogged after him with Brandon beside her. They entered the woods, and their progress slowed. Brambles tore at Emily's jeans, and she had to force her way through the thick tangle of vegetation. Crushed evergreen needles filled the air with pine scent.

The dogs began to bark, then Samson came running back

to Bree with a stick in his mouth. Charley was right behind with a stick as well. "They've found her!" Bree petted her dog. "Show me, Samson."

"Good dog," Emily crooned to Charley. Her heart pounded. So this was the adrenaline high Naomi had said they all felt after a successful search.

Samson, his tail waving proudly, led them toward a stand of white pine trees. The branches drooped close to the ground. Emily couldn't see into the thick branches, but the dog stopped in front of them and barked. He whined and pressed into the branches. Charley raced around the tree, barking as well. There was a heavy scent of pine.

Bree stooped and peered under the trees. "Pansy, are you there?"

She parted the boughs and shined her flashlight into the shadows under them. The eight-year-old girl sat on a bed of pine needles, her eyes red from crying. Bree's voice went soft. "There you are, Pansy. We've been looking for you. Are you trying to stay dry under there? I have a slicker for you." She pulled the yellow plastic garment from her backpack.

Pansy began to cry. "I was scared, Miss Bree. I prayed and prayed you'd bring Samson to find me." She crawled on her hands and knees out from under the trees. Once in the open, she brushed the debris from her jeans. She looked pale, and she was shivering.

Emily whisked a solar blanket from her ready-pack and wrapped it around the little girl, securing it snugly.

"Let's get you back to your mother," Bree said, taking Pansy's hand.

Emily exchanged a smile with Brandon. "Well done," he whispered.

His hand brushed hers. Was it accidental?

As the group exited the woods, the searchlights blazed into the darkness. Emily caught a glint at Brandon's neck. She stared. Her heart thumped faster as blue shimmered under his Adam's apple.

Was that Mrs. Dancer's Sapphire Beauty?

Emily's mouth went dry. She didn't want to believe it, but she was sure it was the necklace. She'd studied it carefully when she'd been making her copy. What Brandon wore sure looked like the original.

Why would Brandon be wearing the missing necklace?

# TWENTY-ONE

The storm rolled out as quickly as it'd rolled in. According to the news Emily had watched earlier in the evening, the weather forecast would be clear and sunny tomorrow. Good thing, since the surfing championship would start in the morning.

She yawned and got up from the sofa. "Night, Dad. Night, Naomi." Timmy and Matthew had gone to bed an hour earlier.

"Wait just a second, honey." He patted the cushion next to him. "There's something I need to tell you."

She eyed his serious expression and sat down between him and Naomi. "What's wrong?"

He glanced at Naomi, then sighed. "There's no way to say it except just to say it. Your mother is out of prison."

Emily sprang to her feet. "What?! You promised, Dad! She can't come back here. She just can't."

Her dad took her hand and tugged her back to the sofa, then put his arm around her. "I'm going to protect you, Emily. You and your brother. I've got a restraining order on her. I don't think she'll come back here."

"She called me, though. She'll come. I know she will." She started to shake, and her eyes filled with tears. She burrowed into the safety of her daddy's arms.

He'd try. She knew he'd do his best. But her mother was sneaky and dangerous.

"I'm going to be watching for her. I'm not going to let her hurt you or Timmy again!"

Naomi scooted over to join in a group hug. "We'll all be careful, honey. And we've warned the sheriff."

"Let's pray together," her dad said.

Emily listened to his deep voice pray for protection for their family. The words comforted her as she lay with her head on her dad's chest. "Amen," she whispered.

Naomi kissed her. "Good night, honey. Rest in God's protection."

Emily nodded. "I will."

She went to her room and shut the door, then tried to relax so she could sleep. Tomorrow would be busy. Unfortunately, her mind wouldn't let her sleep. As if the necklace around Brandon's neck wasn't bad enough, now she had her mother to deal with.

On his little bed beside Emily's, Sherlock whimpered in his sleep as his paws jerked. She smiled. Her puppy probably dreamed of chasing Charley and Samson around. Only a few days in the family and already Emily loved him so much. She couldn't wait to get him enrolled in official training.

Emily rolled onto her back, staring up at the ceiling, and began praying aloud. "God, it's me. Pastor Lukkari told us to talk to you like we do our friends, so that's what I'm doing." She licked her lips. "I know Dad and Naomi want to protect me and Timmy, but I'd sure appreciate it if we didn't have to deal with my mother

at all." She paused, listening to the thunder off in the distance.
"I know your commandment tells me to honor my father *and*
mother, but that's really hard. Especially when honoring one can
mean dishonoring the other. How do I do that? What do I do if
she shows up?"

No booming voice came down from the sky with an answer.

She let out a long sigh and flipped to her side. Maybe God
was trying to get her to figure things out on her own. There was
so much jumbled in her mind: her mother, Timmy's nightmares,
the missing necklace, Mrs. Dancer's reward, Rachel, Brandon,
Sherlock . . . It all tangled into one big knot.

Her cell phone vibrated. She grabbed it and pushed the button to view the text message from Olivia: **u up?**

She texted back: **y**

Her phone rang. "Hey, what's up?" Olivia greeted her.

"You won't believe it."

"What?" She could hear the concern in Olivia's voice.

Emily told her about her mother's parole. "So keep a lookout
with me, okay? I don't want her anywhere near Timmy."

"I will, Em. Wow. But I'm sure your dad is going to protect
you."

"He told the sheriff too."

"That's good. Gosh, it's just one problem after another. Do
you really think Brandon had Mrs. Dancer's necklace on?"

Emily rubbed her eyes and scooted to a semi-sitting position against the pillows propped on the headboard. "I don't really
know now. It was dark, and the storm was rolling in. The searchlights were bright. Too bright." Maybe she'd been wrong.

"But?"

"I don't know." She picked at the Kool-Aid stain on her fleece pajama bottoms. "It looked like it, but then again, so did my copy. I don't want to say anything to him until I'm certain it's the real necklace."

"Are you trying to convince *me* of that, or yourself?"

"I don't know."

A long silence fell over the connection.

"Okay, if it was, why?" Olivia asked.

"I haven't figured that one out."

"I've been thinking."

"Yeah?" Emily could just picture her best friend. Olivia would be sitting cross-legged in her bed, tapping the end of her nose.

"If Mrs. Dancer knew her nephew had taken the necklace, she could offer the reward without worrying about ever having to pay it."

That didn't make a lot of sense. "I'm not following. If she knew Brandon took it, and I'm not saying he did, why would she bother offering a reward in the first place, whether she had to pay it or not?"

"In the beginning, who was your first suspect?"

"Mrs. Dancer."

"Right. And what did you think her motive was?" Olivia asked.

Emily thought about it for a second. "Well, because she got a lot of publicity, which made her stuff sell more. Inetta said it increased her sales. And then Inetta did the second article on her about the reward money, so I imagine her sales picked up again."

"Right. So if she took her own necklace for the publicity, offering a reward didn't matter, because she'd never have to pay it."

"So why do it?"

"To get more attention. Mr. Farmer probably wouldn't have had Inetta do that second interview if she hadn't offered the reward. Nothing new on the case wouldn't have been exactly newsworthy."

True. She had a point. However . . . "But if Brandon took the necklace . . . how does that tie in?"

Olivia let out a heavy breath. "I haven't worked that one out. Maybe it wasn't the Sapphire Beauty but something that just looked like it."

As if Emily hadn't tried to tell herself that a gazillion times? But the truth was, he'd had on the Sapphire Beauty, or a really good imitation. Better than Emily's. "It was. I've tried to reason myself into believing that because I don't want to believe Brandon stole from his own aunt, but I can't. It was the Sapphire Beauty." And tomorrow she'd have to tell Sheriff Kaleva.

But she'd give Brandon the chance to tell the sheriff himself first. She'd give him the opportunity to explain, something no one had given her.

"Well, wh—hang on." Voices muffled. "I gotta go. Mom said if I don't go to bed now, I'll never get up on time to watch the first phase of the competition tomorrow. Night."

"Bye. See you in the morning." Emily set her phone on her bedside table and inched herself back down into the bed.

She closed her eyes, willing herself to relax and go to sleep. She peeked at the clock with one eye: 10:13. Rolling over to her stomach, she punched her pillow underneath her head.

Sherlock whimpered in his sleep again.

Off in the distance, she could barely make out the last echoes of thunder.

Emily checked the clock again: 10:17.

She tossed over onto her side. Tucked the covers under her chin. Rubbed her nose when it started to itch.

Footsteps thudded in the hall. Light spilled from the bathroom. A door clicked shut. A minute. Two. The toilet flushed. Water ran. Light filled the hallway for a second, then only the hall nightlight glowed. More footsteps back to Timmy's room.

Silence.

She snuck another peek at the clock: 10:28.

This was ridiculous. Emily shoved the covers off, was careful not to trip over her sleeping puppy, then headed to the kitchen. Maybe a glass of water would help.

She took a sip from the bottle in the fridge.

A soft whimper made her spin. Sherlock and Charley both stood in the kitchen doorway, Charley sniffing the puppy's head.

"Good boy, Charley, for hearing him." She scooped Sherlock up into her arms. "Do you need to go outside, sweet boy?" She crossed to the back door and unlocked it.

Charley growled.

Emily set Sherlock down. "Well, you can go out with him, Charley."

The dog growled again as the puppy headed over the threshold. Charley barked and shot out the door. He barked again.

Emily's pulse thumped. What if something was in the backyard? Something that could hurt Sherlock? Her heart in her throat, she reached for the floodlights switch. She froze. What if it was the Windigo? Or even worse. *My mother.*

"Honey, what's wrong? I heard Charley." Naomi appeared, the edges of her robe grazing the top of her slippers.

Charley barked again.

Emily jumped.

"Hey, it's okay." Naomi flipped on the lights.

A raccoon jumped off the trash can and headed toward the back fence. Charley barked again. Sherlock, yipping, ran after the coon. Naomi whistled, and Charley immediately went to her. Sherlock raced behind.

"Good boy." Naomi gave Charley a rub behind his ears, then let him inside.

Emily lifted her puppy into her arms and snuggled him against her neck as Dad stepped into the kitchen. "Is something wrong?"

"We're fine, honey. Dogs found a raccoon in the backyard is all."

He frowned. "You're sure that's all it was? I'm going to check." He went out the back door.

"Are you all right?" Naomi asked. "I don't think your mom would have had time to get here."

"I guess you're right. And it wasn't just her. I let my imagination run away with me, I guess. All that talk about the Windigo."

Naomi didn't smile. "You know that's all just a legend, right?"

"Sure."

"Good. Because God has you in his protection. Nothing can happen to you unless it passes through his hands first. You don't need a necklace or anything else when you have God."

Of course Emily knew all that. Still, the reminder was a comfort tonight.

Her dad came back in, but he was frowning. "I saw some footprints. I'm going to call the sheriff. Don't you worry, though, honey. Whoever was out there is gone now."

*My mother?* Emily swallowed hard. "Should I sleep with Timmy?"

Her dad smiled. "You've always taken good care of him, Em.

I'm proud of you. But I'm here, and no one is getting past me. You try to get some rest."

Naomi kissed her cheek. "Tuck Sherlock in good. If he whimpers, just give him the chew toy Bree gave you, and he should fall back to sleep fairly easily."

"Good night." Emily snuggled her puppy as she shut her bedroom door behind her and set Sherlock in his bed.

Footprints. If not her mother, then who? A startling thought hit her: there was no doubt Brandon believed in the Windigo one hundred percent, yet he hadn't been at all uneasy about searching in the woods where the Ojibwa believed the Windigo lived. Matter of fact, when she'd asked him about being too scared to stay with the search for Pansy, he'd said he was perfectly safe. If he had the necklace that he believed could protect him from the Windigo, no wonder he hadn't been worried.

Emily crawled into bed, nearly sick to her stomach. She had no choice but to tell Sheriff Kaleva tomorrow. She could only pray Brandon had a logical explanation for everything.

And that he'd forgive her for her suspicions.

The sun rose brightly on Saturday morning, just as the meteorologist predicted. Emily was glad. The surf team had practiced hard and deserved to compete. It'd be awesome if they could win.

She hopped out of the Honda SUV and waited while Dad and Naomi got Timmy and Matthew out, then the large blanket. Too bad they'd had to leave Sherlock at home, but Charley bounded around, not seeming to be constrained by his leash in the least.

The waves rolled in with a resounding crash every few minutes—a perfect day for surfing if you liked frigid water. The sections just behind the roped-off area were already filled with beach blankets and lawn chairs as people settled in for good placement to watch the surfers.

For once, Emily was glad Timmy hadn't been able to find his shoes. If they had arrived any earlier, they would've gotten a closer seat. About twelve feet from the yellow rope was close enough for her. She had no desire to feel the spray of the lake on her face.

She caught sight of Olivia and her parents. "Dad, can I go hang with Olivia?"

He nodded. "Okay. Mason said your mother is not in the area, and I don't think she'll show her face, but just in case, keep your cell on, don't wander off, and—"

"Answer if you or Naomi call." Emily grinned. "I got it, Dad."

He smiled. "Have fun."

She ran over to her best friend. "Hi, Mr. and Mrs. Webster. How was your cruise?"

Olivia's mom's blond hair lifted in the breeze. "It was wonderful. Just what we needed. I have some little gifts for you and your parents and brothers. I'll bring them to church tomorrow." Her blue eyes sparkled under the bright sun.

"You didn't have to do that." But how cool—presents from a cruise.

"We just wanted to thank you for letting Olivia stay with you."

"That was fun." Emily grinned at her best friend. "Olivia's like my sister, you know."

Mrs. Webster smiled. "I know."

"Mom, can I go with Emily? We want to go wish the team good luck."

"Sure. Stay together and keep your cell phone on."

"Yes, ma'am."

They passed Mayor Kaleva on the sidewalk. She and her daughter, Zoe, were handing out flyers to every person who passed.

They walked across the beach, wet sand kicking up behind them as they made their way to where the competitors warmed up. It didn't take them long to find the Gitchee Gumee Surfers in their new, logoed wet suits. Brandon smiled in their direction as they approached.

Again, Emily's stomach knotted. How could she accuse him of having the necklace? She knew what it felt like to be accused of something you didn't do.

But she'd seen the necklace. She knew it was the missing Sapphire Beauty.

At least she was giving him a chance to explain. His aunt hadn't given her a chance. Emily could only pray she was doing the right thing.

She should be happy that her name would soon be cleared. But she wasn't. Not when doing so would ruin Brandon's reputation. Especially since everyone knew he had his heart set on applying to Stanford in California. It was one of the best schools in the country, and it had an awesome surf team. With his grades, it was the talk of Rock Harbor that he'd not only be accepted but probably win a good scholarship.

What would this do to his future?

# TWENTY-TWO

The fog rolled in after the second heat of competition, right after Josh had surfed. Emily shivered as she zipped her jacket. The announcer called for the third-wave competitors. Emily grabbed Olivia's arm. "This is Brandon's group."

The horn blasted. Six surfers paddled out into the surf. Brandon's blue team shirt stood out against the water lapping the surfers' boards.

"Our team is ahead by seven points after the first two heats. If we can pick up another two points for the lead, there's no way we won't place."

*God, maybe it's wrong to pray for a certain team to win in a competition, but I sure hope we win.* For the team. Yeah, and if she was being honest, for Brandon too.

A wave started in the back of the lineup, gaining speed and height as its crest shoved toward Brandon. The drop was particularly fierce. He glanced over his shoulder to gauge his position, then began paddling. He duck-dove.

Emily squeezed Olivia's arm.

Brandon popped up and straightened on his board, catching the wave in the middle and maneuvering to the shoulder of the breaking wave. He executed a perfect floater off the lip, then cut back before demonstrating a classical top-turn.

The rest of the Gitchee Gumee Surfers screamed, hollered, and whistled. Emily found herself jumping up and down along with the crowd as the announcer called out the maneuvers over the loudspeaker.

"And now the blue surfer looks like he's going to catch a tube. Here it comes . . . can he hit it?"

Emily held her breath.

"And he's caught it. Look at that tube ride."

The people littering the beach stood, clapping and hollering. After what felt like an hour to Emily, when actually it was mere minutes, Brandon's ride was over. And so was the heat.

"He had to have pulled in two more points than the other teams. That was awesome," Olivia said as they waited for the scores to be announced.

Emily watched Brandon high-five his teammates after retiring his board and getting a clap on the back from Coach Larson. He ducked into the tent the surfers used to change. Minutes later he emerged in sweatpants and a team logo shirt and spoke with the coach.

Olivia's cell phone rang. "Hey, Mom. Did you see that? Our team is definitely going to win now."

Emily tuned out her friend's half of the call as Brandon turned in her direction. He smiled at her, and her face heated.

Brandon said something to the coach before grabbing another towel and rubbing it over his head.

"Yes, ma'am." Olivia shoved the phone into her jacket pocket.

"Hey, Mom needs me to bring her one of Mayor Kaleva's flyers. I'll be right back, okay?"

Emily nodded absentmindedly as Brandon tossed the towel in the bin and jogged in her direction. She barely registered her best friend running off.

"What a ride, huh?" Brandon's eyes were like dark Hershey's chocolates. "The coach thinks this will put us over the top."

"It's awesome." Why couldn't she think of something clever to say?

He turned as his score was announced: 9.3! The other teams couldn't catch the Gitchee Gumee Surfers now! His teammates whooped and hollered, screaming his name. He pumped his fist in the air, then without warning, grabbed Emily in a bear hug. He lifted her off the ground and twirled her around.

Her breath caught sideways in her throat.

Brandon set her down. "Sorry. But do you realize we just won the competition?"

She nodded as she worked to catch her balance. She smiled up at him, then froze as her eyes went to the leather cord peeping out from his shirt around his neck. A cord that looked just like the one she used for her copy of the Sapphire Beauty. One just like Mary Dancer used.

Emily reached up and grabbed the cord, pulling the necklace from the shirt. The fused glass caught in the sunlight fighting against the fog. She gasped as she dropped the necklace against his chest.

No denying he had the Sapphire Beauty now.

"I can explain."

"I hope so, because I have to tell the sheriff." She turned, striding toward the hordes of people huddled on the beach.

"Emily, wait." He grabbed her elbow. "Please. Just come with me, and I'll explain everything." His tanned face had gone two shades paler.

She chewed her bottom lip. Mrs. Dancer and the sheriff hadn't really given her much opportunity to explain. Then again, she'd been innocent. Brandon wasn't. The proof hung around his neck.

"Please, just hear me out. I didn't steal it. Just hear me out. In private. If this gets out, I'll never be able to get into a good college."

"What do you mean, you didn't steal it? You're wearing it! I don't understand." But she wouldn't want to be the reason he was in trouble if he was innocent. "Okay, I'll listen."

Brandon kept his hand under her elbow and led her away from the beach, up toward town. He kept a steady hold on her as they passed the tavern and ducked down an alley.

She dug in her heels. "I don't want to go any farther."

"I don't want to be overheard." He yanked on her arm and half dragged her deeper behind the storefronts. She took in a deep breath as they stopped in back of Rock Harbor Savings and Loan.

Brandon turned to face her. "I know what you must think."

Emily crossed her arms over her chest. How could he know what she thought when she didn't even know what she thought?

"I didn't steal the necklace. Aunt Mary gave it to my mother."

"I don't understand. You mean your aunt had it all along?"

Brandon fingered the necklace and nodded. "Aunt Mary needed to sell more of her jewelry because the bank threatened to foreclose on her house. She couldn't afford to run any ads in the paper or anything, so she decided she'd report her necklace missing from the festival. It would give her publicity and probably up her sales with people wanting to own something that was worth enough to be stolen."

Emily's mouth went drier. "She set me up?" It was hard for her to imagine that the lady whose talent she'd admired for years would set her up.

Brandon shook his head. "You were never part of the deal, at least from what I understand. Aunt Mary planned to report the necklace missing, but she didn't even know your booth was going to be beside hers." He rested a heavy hand on her shoulder.

She shrugged it off. "But she didn't just report it missing, Brandon. She put my copy in its place." The memory of Mrs. Dancer's glare made her burn from the inside out. "She even went so far as to suggest I only made a replica because I'd planned to steal hers." The sheriff sure seemed to give that some serious consideration too.

"That wasn't planned, as far as I know, Emily."

"So she just took advantage of the opportunity? Made my parents think I was irresponsible or a thief?" Anger slipped into her blood. "Accepted my earnings my parents made me give her while all the time she had the necklace?"

"I'm so sorry, Emily. Really, I am. You weren't supposed to be involved."

"What was she going to do? She couldn't very well sell the necklace, not with the police looking for it."

His eyes pleaded with her to understand. "Her plan was to take it apart and just make other pieces with the fused glass and beads."

Emily pointed to his necklace. "Apparently she didn't."

"My mother saw it the next day. She recognized it from the

picture in the paper."

"And?"

"Well, Mom confronted her about it. Mom never wanted her to sell it in the first place—it was blessed so it should stay in the tribe. Aunt Mary explained how the bank was going to take her house. She begged Mom to keep quiet. What could Mom say? That's her sister."

Well, Emily could understand . . . kinda. She wouldn't want Timmy to lose his house. But that still didn't explain him wearing the necklace. "So why didn't she take it apart like she'd originally planned?"

"Aunt Mary had the necklace blessed by some of our tribal leaders. It truly is blessed with protection against the Windigo. If the necklace was taken apart, the protection would be gone. Any pieces she tried to reuse would prevent any further blessing from that new item."

"You really believe that Windigo stuff?"

Brandon nodded. "I told you I believe in good and evil."

"God is good, not some enchantment charm on some necklace. Windigos aren't real. Evil, real evil, is sin."

Brandon shook his head. "My elders wouldn't say the Windigo was real unless it was true. And this necklace did protect me. Like the night we searched and found the kid."

"That necklace had nothing to do with any protection, Brandon." The more she talked, the more certain she was that everything she'd been taught was true. "God loves us all. He protects us. He made sure that we found Pansy and returned safely. Not a stupid necklace. The Bible tells us not to make idols like that but to put our trust and faith in God."

Brandon didn't look at all convinced. But she couldn't make

someone accept the truth. "So why did your aunt give your mom the necklace anyway? Wasn't she worried someone would see it, like I did?"

"Mom told Aunt Mary she wanted to give it to me, knowing the competition was coming up and that some of our elders had said the Windigo was on the prowl. They both wanted to make sure I was protected."

"What your aunt did was wrong. Lying about something being stolen is fraud. It's a crime. And you and your mom not saying anything, that was wrong too."

"It's not so bad. I mean, nobody got hurt. Nobody lost anything."

That made her angry. "It hurt me and my reputation. I lost the money I'd made at the festival—my dad made me give it to your aunt because her necklace went missing while I was responsible for it."

"I'll pay you back." Brandon took a step closer to her.

She shook her head. "My reputation got hurt. People thought I might have something to do with it."

"Not really. Everyone knows what a goody-goody you are."

Her face grew hotter. Was that how people thought of her? As a goody-goody? Well, maybe she was. "That doesn't matter, Brandon. It's wrong."

Her cell phone rang. She fished it out of her jacket pocket and glanced at the caller ID. It was Olivia.

Brandon snatched it from her hand before she could answer.

"Give me back my phone." She reached for it, but he raised it over her head.

She curled her hands into fists at her side. "I said, give it back."

"You have to agree not to say anything. I'll get your money back, I promise." He sounded desperate.

She took a step toward him. "Give me my phone. Now."

He turned off the phone. "Let it go, Emily. Seriously. Just let it go." His face twisted. "I'm not going to let you mess up my future."

Suddenly she wasn't sure about him. *Oh, God, I don't know what to do. He's scaring me. I don't know what to say. Please help me. Nobody knows where I am. I need your help.*

She grabbed her phone from his grip but didn't take the time to turn it back on. There was no telling what he'd do. "Brandon, you have to do the right thing. No matter what. Lying is wrong, even if it's for family." She took two steps backward, toward the mouth of the alley. "God loves you, and he'll take care of you, but you have to do what's right."

Brandon didn't say anything, just stared at her like she'd grown another head. "I can't tell anyone or the Windigo will come for me. My aunt knows about these things, and she told me what it would do."

Her mouth went dry. "One of my favorite Bible verses is Psalm 106:3: 'Blessed are those who act justly, who always do what is right.' That means God blesses those who do what's right. You need to tell Sheriff Kaleva the truth. What your aunt did. The truth. All of it."

He shook his head. "I'll get into a lot of trouble. I'll probably get kicked off the surf team, and there's no way I'll get into a college like Stanford with a criminal record."

"Maybe you won't get in trouble. Your aunt is to blame for this—not you. Sure, you should have told someone, but just wearing the necklace isn't a crime. You have the chance to come forward on your own. That will account for a lot, I think." She turned and headed toward the beach.

Brandon stepped in front of her. "You can't tell anyone."

Fear gripped her by the throat, but she couldn't show it. "I have to tell the truth, Brandon. And you should want to."

He reached out, grabbing her arm. Her heart beat double time.

The foghorn sounded out across the water, and the sound sent shivers up Emily's spine. "Please, Brandon, you need to do the right thing here." She pulled away from his tight grip, and he let her go.

She pointed at the necklace around his neck. "That won't protect you from God's disapproval. What you and your aunt did was wrong. You need to tell the sheriff the truth."

He hesitated. "I can't bring shame to my family."

"There's no shame in telling the truth. You aunt is the one who should be ashamed."

His face worked, and he swallowed hard. "I don't know what to do." He looked like he was about to cry.

A bark came behind her, and she whirled to see Samson running full speed toward her. He skidded to a stop in front of her and leaped onto her leg with his tail wagging fast enough to make a breeze. Well, almost.

She fell to her knees and threw her arms around him. "My family will be right behind him, you know." Moments later Charley arrived and went into a near spasm of joy at finding her. She endured the licks and excitement.

Brandon backed away and turned toward the other end of the alley as if to run.

"Don't run, Brandon," she said. "Be brave and face this. Tell Sheriff Kaleva what really happened. If you don't, I will."

He hesitated for a long moment, then covered his face with his hands. "You're right. I shouldn't have gotten involved in this. I knew all along it was wrong. I'm so sorry you were accused, Emily."

Bree's voice came from down Kitchigami. "Samson!"

Emily released the hero of a dog, and he seized a stick, then ran off. He would lead them here in moments. Charley wasn't about to leave her. Dusting off her hands, she rose and stood by Brandon. "I'll help you."

His shoulders sagged. "What will they do to me?"

"I don't know, but it's not like you stole it. Your aunt owned it and gave it to your mom, who gave it to you."

"I'm an accessory though, right?"

"You're a kid. And it was your family." She was trying to encourage herself as much as him. She knew that there was a chance he could get in big trouble for this.

Samson barked, and Bree, with Naomi beside her, emerged out of the fog. The sheriff followed on their heels.

Naomi broke into a run and reached her first. She threw her arms around Emily and hugged her tight. Emily's face was smashed into Naomi's shoulder, smelling of woods and dog.

"I'm fine, Naomi," she said, her voice muffled by Naomi's jacket. "Brandon didn't hurt me. He just wanted to talk."

Naomi released her, and her brows gathered in a fierce frown. "This wasn't like a date, was it?"

Emily's cheeks felt like they were on fire. "No, no, nothing like that." If she'd ever even thought about it before, she definitely couldn't now.

Brandon stepped forward. "Emily's trying to protect me, Mrs. O'Reilly, but I can't let her. I did kind of force her to come with me." He tugged on the necklace around his neck. "She saw this, and I wanted to talk her into keeping quiet about it."

"The necklace?" Sheriff Kaleva asked with a hand on his holster belt. "You took the necklace?"

He shook his head. "Not exactly."

Emily couldn't stand to watch him struggle. "His aunt took her own necklace for the publicity. She was going to recycle the glass and make something else, but Brandon's mom talked her out of it."

The sheriff put his hand on her shoulder gently. "Let him talk, Emily."

She hung her head. "Sorry."

Brandon took off the necklace and stared at it. "It's blessed, and my mom didn't want my aunt to mess with the magic." He held out his hand. "Here's the necklace. I wanted to say something, but I was afraid. My aunt told me that the Windigo would come for me if I told anyone. And I didn't want to get my aunt into trouble."

The sheriff took the necklace from Brandon and dropped it into his front shirt pocket.

Emily clenched her hands together. "He couldn't really turn in his own family, Sheriff. You don't have to arrest him, do you?"

The sheriff hesitated, then shook his head. "It was his aunt's property, and she gave it to his mother, who gave it to him. If anyone did something illegal, it was his aunt for filing a fake police report." The sheriff took off his hat and rubbed his hair. "I guess I'd best go arrest Mary Dancer for filing a false police report." He stared hard at the boy. "It says a lot that you told the truth now. I'll make sure the DA knows you told me what really happened."

Brandon sagged with visible relief. "Thanks, Sheriff. And my mom?"

"We'll see what the DA says. I hope you know better than to do something like this again, Brandon."

"I do, sir. Absolutely."

The sheriff glanced at Naomi and Bree. "I assume you can handle this from here and get Emily home. Brandon, come with me."

"How did you know to look for me?" Emily asked as she watched Brandon walk off with the sheriff.

Naomi kept her arm around her. "When you weren't where Olivia left you and you didn't answer her call, she came and told us. We immediately sent the dogs looking. We were a little worried that your mother had found you."

Emily shivered, then sighed. "I'm really glad it wasn't her. You know, Brandon is hoping to apply to Stanford. This could kill his chances. It'd definitely put him out of the running for a scholarship. We need to pray for him."

"I will, honey." Naomi hugged her yet again. "I'm so glad you're okay. I'll call your dad and let him know." She walked a few feet away with her cell phone in her hand.

Now that it was all over, Emily was exhausted. She sank onto a rock. Samson came to push his head into her hands, and she rubbed his ears.

Bree stepped a few feet closer. "I'm so proud of you, Em."

Emily looked up. "Really?"

Bree nodded. "You were really brave today."

It meant a lot coming from Bree. Emily straightened and smiled. Her name was cleared, but right now all she wanted to do was get home and go to bed.

This whole adventure thing had turned out pretty well. Now she wanted to focus on training Sherlock and hanging out with her friends. Wait until Olivia heard the whole story. She was going to seriously freak.

# EPILOGUE

The evening air whooshed around the backyard as Sherlock chased the ball Emily tossed. Timmy and Dad laughed at the puppy's clumsiness. Bree and Naomi sat on the picnic table with Emily.

"Here you go, Bree." Emily leaned across the picnic table and counted out the money into Bree's hand. "That will take care of training Sherlock. I'm excited to get started."

Bree sighed and tucked the money into her wallet. "I wish you'd let me teach you for free. I don't want to take your money."

Emily glanced at Naomi. "It's the responsible thing to do."

Mary Dancer had paid back the money she'd accepted from Emily, though she was still in trouble for filing a fake report, and it felt good to be able to hand the cash over to Bree. And Brandon wasn't in any serious trouble. As far as Emily knew, nothing would go on his permanent record. If he didn't get into Stanford, it wouldn't be because she'd gotten him busted.

Bree snapped her fingers and called Samson to her side. "It's getting late. Kade will be wondering if the Windigo got me." She winked at Emily.

Emily wanted to sink into the grass. Did everyone know how stupid she'd been about that dumb Windigo? "See you at training on Saturday."

She waited until Bree and Samson got in the SUV. "Thank you again, Naomi. For Sherlock. For helping me. For everything."

"You're welcome. I love you, Emily."

"I love you too." She smiled as Sherlock tripped over his own feet. Timmy lay on the ground beside the puppy, letting the dog's tongue wash his cheeks.

Dad turned and winked at Emily, then sat on the other side of Naomi, reaching for her hand.

Her heart pounded in her chest. She loved her family. Matthew. Dad. Naomi. And Timmy, even when he annoyed her.

Emily closed her eyes. *Thank you, God. My life's looking pretty good right now. And if my mother shows up, Dad will deal with her.*

She opened her eyes as Sherlock jumped against her leg.

Yep, her life was pretty good indeed.

# ACKNOWLEDGMENTS

## *FROM COLLEEN*

I can't imagine doing a joint Rock Harbor project with anyone but Robin. We first became friends when she emailed me after reading *Without a Trace*. It was super fun to do this together!

Thanks to the great team at Tommy Nelson! It was a dream come true to get to do this book with you! I look forward to my granddaughter Alexa reading it one day.

My special thanks to my great husband who took the added workload in stride the way he does everything. And as always, I'm in awe of what doors God has opened for me and thank him daily for his blessings in my life.

## *FROM ROBIN*

My most heartfelt thanks to my dear friend, prayer warrior, and mentor, Colleen, who came to me with this project and asked if I was interested. This has been such a blessing to work with you . . . and I am grateful you allowed me to play with some of my favorite people—the characters from Rock Harbor.

As for the publishing team at Tommy Nelson, I could not have asked for a better group of talented folks who welcomed me into their fold. Special thanks to Mac and Molly, for all your suggestions and editing.

As always, there are many in the writing community who help me in so many ways, I can't even begin to name the ways. My heartfelt thanks to: Pam Hillman, Ronie Kendig, Tosca Lee, Dineen Miller, Cara Putman, and Cheryl Wyatt.

My extended family members are my biggest fans and greatest cheerleaders. Thank you for ALWAYS being in my corner: Mom and Papa, BB and Robert, Bek and Krys, Bubba and Lisa, Brandon, and Rachel.

I couldn't do what I do without my girls—Emily Carol, Remington Case, and Isabella Co-Ceaux. I love each of you so much! Thank y'all so much for everything. And my precious grandsons, Benton and Zayden. You are joys in my life. There aren't enough words to express the love and gratitude for my husband, Case. Thank you for putting up with my moods, deadline insanity, and for following me into the crazy industry and loving it. I could not do this without you and I love you with all my heart.

Finally, all glory to my Lord and Savior, Jesus Christ. *I can do all things through Him who gives me strength.*